Gifts and Flowers Sent My Way: Loving a Thug on Valentines Day

By: Author Tina Marie

Acknowledgements

I would first like to thank God for giving me this gift of writing and for providing me with every blessing I have received this far and will receive in the future.

I want to thank my family, my fiancé Jay for putting up with all the late nights and my crazy moods while I am writing. To my kids Jashanti, Jaymarni and Jasheer I want you to know that I work so hard so you can have it all. I want to thank all of my Pen Sisters no matter what company you are in for all of the love, support and for always helping to push me to my next goal, I appreciate you all.

To the crew, my sisters, Sharome, Shante, and Andrea I just want to say I love you all. Ladora you are the world's best little sister I love you and I believe in you keep pushing that number 1 is coming your way. Demetrea you are always there when I need to vent, cry or celebrate and I would do anything for you, love you lots!

To my Bad & Boujie team you came into my life at a time when I felt like I was alone in this writing ish. I guess God knew who I needed and when. I love you ladies to the moon and back. Thanks for all the calls, texts, laughter and tears and for showing me the definition of real friends. (I know all ya'll thug asses crying).

A special thank you to Tyanna for being a constant sweetheart and motivator. Chanique J for always having my back and my front, and Author Natavia, for being my friend, and one of my favorite authors all in one. Rikenya you have such a pure and kind heart, you are the kind of friend to be cherished and I do cherish you.

Nisey, I just have to say, Sis, you're the best. You know my schedule better than me and make me stick to it and never allow me to make excuses. Quanisha, you're a bomb assistant/admin. You don't let me forget a thing and handle all the grunt work so I can write. Love you, boo. Keke you have become my life line and even when your bossy I still love you. Sweets there would be no book without you, even when you told me to rewrite a whole chapter I still loved you! Keri this book is for you boo!!! I hope you love how your character turned out!

To Zatasha and all the Bookies I appreciate the love and support you show all authors not just me. It makes a difference having a place where we are respected, celebrated and offered endless support!

To my friends and family: I appreciate all of the love and support. My cousins, Dionne, Donna & Tanisha. My friends: Letitia, Natasha, Jennifer, Diana and Kia. I'm truly grateful for you all, and I love you. And to my best friend there will never be enough letters in the alphabet to thank you.

To all of my fans, readers, test readers, admins and anyone who has ever read or purchased my work, shared a link or a book cover, you're all appreciated, and I promise to keep pushing on your behalf to write what you're looking for.

Chapter 1

Shaquita

"Ahhh, Mom help he's killing him," Ray Ray yelled from the other side of the door, loud as fuck as always. My friend shot up in the bed with a concerned look on his face. I shook my head hoping Ray Ray would shut the fuck up so this nigga would relax, and we could get back to us. I swear since Shakita went to live with my pops these kids have gotten ten times worse. I jumped up in only my black lace thong and cracked the bedroom door open.

"Ma he's torturing the class hamster. The teacher told me I was in charge of the class hamster and now Boobie's going to kill him." Ray Ray stood there holding an empty cage. "Ma he is so fucked up. You need to lock him away. He said he was going to pull Teddy's little hands and feet off," Ray Ray cried out with tears in his eyes. His face was swollen from crying and he had his fists bawled up at his side.

"Boy you better go figure that shit out. You're the oldest and you need to control Boobie, not allow him to control you. Now shut up because you're interrupting my good time. Take your brother outside and leave me be," I hissed trying to keep my voice down. Turning around I forced a smile onto my face for EJ as I slow walked to the bed. I made sure to climb over him so he got a face full of my boobs and a good look at my ass. "Sorry babe my sons like to play around but they won't be bothering us again." I could see the look of disgust on his face when I said my sons. That was why EJ was my latest project. He was literally perfect for what I had in mind. He hated kids, had a shit load of money and was addicted to my pussy. Soon enough he would be joining Julian, Darren and Raymond in what I called team baby daddy.

I let my hand roam down to his hard dick so we could pick up where we left off. He quickly got over the interruption and I took comfort in the fact that I heard the front door slam, letting me know the kids had left the house. I laughed to myself as he grabbed the condom from the bedside table. I had so many holes in those condoms he would be raining sperm all in my pussy. Just like every time we got together.

We had been going at it all night and my pussy was sore but me and her had a pep talk this morning. I told her to suck it up since I was ovulating and needed all the opportunity I could to get pregnant and trap EJ. Climbing on top of him I rocked my hips back and forth enjoying the feel of a hard dick inside of me. Shit nothing wrong with enjoying a good plan. "Yes girl you got that snap back pussy," he moaned while squeezing his eyes closed like a bitch. I popped my pussy a little harder and ran my hands over his chest urging him to nut inside of me. As soon as his body stiffened the bedroom door flew open.

"This is the shit we do Eric James Williams," an angry female yelled as she walked in my room and snatched me by my ponytail. I flew in the air pussy juices splashing everyone close by, including her. I felt the hard wood floor against my bare back and ass as she dropped me like a bag of trash. Damn she was strong to be so little. Her light brown skin had turned an odd color of purple as she punched EJ in the face. "You leave our bed and home where our kids lay their heads and come fuck this bitch," she shouted looking down at me.

I wanted to fight back but fuck it, I really wasn't shit and that was cool with me. Plus, I had already executed the plan, so it was probably already too late for EJ and his family. Wow a whole wife and kids, he sure had me fooled. This baby we were going to have was going to have his ass feeling the same way, fooled.

EJ jumped up not saying shit just putting on his clothes faster than a fire fighter jumping in his suit. He grabbed for the crazy girl who I assumed was his wife from the size of the rock on her hand. Before he could get a hold on her we all jumped as a huge crash was heard and I suddenly felt a breeze from outside. It sounded like a bulldozer hit my shit.

Grabbing a sheet to cover in I ran down the stairs speechless at the red Cadillac sitting in my living room. Well, not a bulldozer but close enough. Boobie was in the driver's seat grinning from ear to ear, his brother sat next to him with a blank look. "What the hell, your kid just crashed my car," the unknown woman screeched. For the first time ever I really didn't have words to describe the scene before me. The spot where my TV used to be was filled with a car instead. I had to tell myself that a few good times before I truly could wrap my head around it. I had blocked out all the shit EJ's wife was saying to try and figure out what to do next.

Suddenly I felt my arms being grabbed roughly by a strong grip. "Yo what the fuck is wrong with your kid's ma? I hope you know you about to pay for my shorties car." EJ stood before me with a look colder than the freezing air from outside. After a few more shakes he flung me to the side and picked up his raging girl. "What kind of mother sends their kids outside in the winter to play anyway," he shot at me as he made his way to the door. The look on his face was a familiar one. It was the same one that Chrome used to wear anytime he was in the presence of my kids. Disbelief filled with disgust.

I missed Chrome, so far, he was true to his word and has not even been by for a fuck and suck special. I tried to call him lots of times but he must have had me blocked because it always went right to voicemail. I heard how he and Kyona had a baby. Every time I saw her at work I wanted to slit her throat because she had easily achieved what I worked so hard for.

Suddenly I realized I was all alone with a car in my living room and my pussy feeling the cold air from outside. I started laughing out loud at the situation, I laughed so hard that I ended up doubled over clutching my sheet. I needed a to pop a perk asap to make it through this shit. My laughter was interrupted by a knock at the front door. Why the hell was someone knocking on the door when there was a huge hole in the wall? That just made me laugh harder.

Stepping over the debris I opened the door with an amused look on my face that quickly faded when met with the shiny gold badge on the other side. "Ma'am what is going on here," the first officer said as he stepped inside causing me to flatten myself against the wall or be trampled. If he didn't look amused his partner seriously missed the joke, she was looking me up and down like I was dog shit on her shoe. "Rachel, call an ambulance we have an injured child in the car," he shouted running over and opening the doors of the Cadillac. Honestly in all the chaos with EJ and the shock of hearing that he had a wife I had forgotten all about the kids. *Fuck.*

Ray Ray had a gash in his head that was bleeding a lot. I knew from experience with these heathens that it probably looked worse than it actually was, shit head wounds bled a lot. His eyes were glossy and he was shaking in the officers arms. These kids loved the dramatics. I wondered where the hell Boobie had disappeared too, since he deiced to turn my house into a scene out of Grand Theft Auto. I wanted to go upstairs and find Mister Feel Good- that's what I named my vibrator and finish the nut these jokers interrupted. Not pretend to care about my bad ass kids.

"Sir, I'm sure they are just fine. It was a minor accident. A woman who I do not personally know left her car running outside while she came into my home and attacked me. I'm suffering from the shock of the whole situation so please forgive me." I slowly made my way over to Ray Ray and began putting on a show of concern. "Baby are you ok," I asked in a low voice placing my hand on his arm? "Mommy is going to take you to the hospital and get you checked out." Boobie picked that time to crawl from the backseat, a grin on his face.

"These are your children," the officer asked outrage clear in his voice? I nodded as I pulled Ray Ray closer to me hoping these nosey ass jakes would just leave. I sent Boobie a silent message with my eyes letting him know I was fucking him up later. "Please step away from the child, help is on the way. And as for you, we will be opening an investigation." Before I could protest that this shit wasn't my fault I heard an engine shut off and a car door slam. I could see the familiar all black Range Rover with the custom plates J1S-FLY and I felt my belly cramp. Visions of Mister Feel good quickly evaporated from my mind. Watching Shakita's father Julian slam the door to his truck and make his way up to the walkway I knew this was not going to be a good day.

Keisha

One year, one week and four days, that was how long it had been since my supposed best friend attacked me with a bat. All because I was telling her the truth, I guess the old saying the truth hurts was for real. I was hurt for a few months after. Every moment since then was spent plotting and planning my revenge. I would still see her at work sometimes and I would smile and nod like everything was cool. I learned a long time ago revenge was really only about playing certain roles to get what you came for.

The fool that Shaquita was, had her walking around like nothing was wrong. Last week she called me asking to go to some new club with her, it took everything in me not to laugh in her face. She really didn't know me at all if she thought I was taking what she did lying down or that we would ever be friends again.

I didn't realize how much patience true revenge actually took. I could have found her the next day and returned the beating but that was just reactionary. What I had planned would do more than leave her with bruised ribs, a broken knee and a fractured arm like she did me. I was going to break her spirit, damage her soul and shatter her world.

"Babe what has you in such a good mood today," my kid's father asked as he rolled over and began playing with my full breasts. I wasn't really into it but I knew if I resisted him he would start crying about me cheating and shit. I mean hell yea I have cheated on him plenty of times and with ease but right now all I wanted was Shaquita's downfall. Ceaser and all of his bullshit was the last thing on my mind. I pulled myself up on the pillows so he had more access to my body and began focusing on the task at hand. "Yea I knew you wanted this dick girl," he murmured to himself smacking me in the face with his cock. Like a good girl I opened wide allowing him to slide into my wet mouth. Even though I was rolling my eyes at the same damn time.

I slurped on his shit and enjoyed the feeling of his dick sliding to the back of my throat. I felt my pussy get wet and knew I was soaking the sheets. His long fingers found their way to my jewel and began stroking my clit with expertise and just like that the little hoe that lives inside of me came running out. Cease was a good fuck, that was one of the reasons I kept him around this long. I mean we had been kicking it since high school and two kids later I knew he wasn't going anywhere and honestly neither was I.

I learned a long time ago consistency meant more than love. I loved someone once, but nothing good came out of it. Feeling the pre cum on my tongue I struggled to push thoughts of "him" out of my mind. Sometimes I forgot the pain of loving him, of wanting him to love me and the ultimate pain of just not being good enough.

"Yes baby catch all this nut," Cease moaned as I jerked my head to the side, so he came all over my face. "Yo why the fuck you move, you think you're too good to swallow my nut? You the kind of girl who should be happy that I would even allow you to suck my shit up. Dumb ass." He didn't even bother to fuck me just jumped off the bed and went to the bathroom so he could leave. Dealing with this nigga was so draining. Hearing tiny feet in the hallway I hurried and wiped myself up and threw on some clothes to go and start my day.

"Hey princess what are you doing up so early?" I asked my six-year-old daughter Cadence, as she smiled up at me. She was missing her two front teeth but it didn't take away from her beauty. I held out my arms so she could jump up and give me a hug like she did every morning. Hearing the downstairs door slam shut I realized her bitch ass daddy didn't even stop to see if she was good. "Come on lets go get your brother before he tears the house apart." Walking into the room my kids shared, my son was sitting up in his twin bed rubbing his eyes. Julian was my only son, my baby and he looked just like his father the only man I ever loved.

Chapter 2

Kyona

When I walked in the barbershop and saw Chrome standing there I felt my heart drop. I never got over him but the fact that I hadn't told him about his daughter made me want to turn and run the other way. When he surprisingly apologized instead of strangling me I was tempted to give in, very tempted. Hell I missed everything about him, his touch, his smell and definitely that donkey sized dick. But I knew it couldn't work. He threw me away when I needed him and I couldn't ever allow a man to hurt me that way again. Plus, with two kids I needed all my focus to be on them, so I ignored my heart and walked away. Now I spent every day since then wondering if I made the right decision.

"Mommy I miss Chrome can you call him to pick me up," Xayden asked me holding my phone in his hand and giving me a puppy dog face. This shit was a daily occurrence since he saw him before Christmas and I was getting tired of it.

"Xay I'm sure that Chrome is busy, and he will see you when he has time." His lip quivered and crocodile tears slid down his face. Serina chose that moment to cry so I didn't have time to baby Xayden. He would just have to get used to Chrome being around some of the time and not all the time. "Stop crying Xay, Tyler will be over soon and said he will play Mario Kart with you while mommy cooks." I said trying to lighten the blow.

He stuck out his tongue at me and stomped his feet, "I

hate Tyler he's boring and he's not my daddy. Chrome is my daddy and he told me I don't need anyone else. So, I don't need Tyler," he yelled in his tiny angry voice as he ran away. Lord, Chrome was still finding ways to make my life difficult even when he wasn't around.

By the time I finished changing the baby my doorbell was ringing. Sitting her in the bright pink and yellow swing I went to let Tyler in. We had been dating exclusively for a few months now and I wish I could say it was love but really he was just someone to keep me company. I vowed to have a talk with my heart about letting him in and shutting Chrome completely out.

"Hey honey," he greeted me kissing me on my cheek. He was dressed like he was off to an evening at church or he was working with the Jehovah's Witnesses. I almost expected him to hand me a pamphlet about Jesus. His sweater vest was the color of green puke and his black dress pants were as stiff as cardboard. I bet if he took them off they would stand up all by themselves. Looking him over one last time I offered a bland smile in place of the laughter that I had to work hard to hold in before I went back to making my roasted chicken and vegetables. "Where is Ayden so we can play his game?" He asked saying my sons name wrong as always. I wanted to snap on his ass, like damn nigga we been knowing each other for damn near two years and you still couldn't remember my sons name. Before I could speak my mind I was interrupted by banging on my door. Who the fuck now?

Snatching open the door I was so shocked I almost swallowed my tongue. "Man move the fuck out my way shorty," Chrome said as he shoved his way past me and into my house. "Where my son at," he asked as he moved further inside. "Xayden, let's go," he yelled up the stairs while grilling the shit out of me. How the hell did he even know where I lived? I moved before I had Serina because I needed more space, and I specifically did not make my location available to Chrome.

Looking at Chrome I was in awe of him, causing my anger to be forgotten for the moment. He looked so sexy in his olive green Timbs, Versace Jeans and black North Face. He hadn't shaved in a few days and the slight beard made him look even meaner than usual. I was so busy staring at him I hadn't even noticed Tyler had walked up beside me until he lightly touched my shoulder. "Are you ok Ky," he asked low enough so only I could hear? Well damn I hope I was ok because his little soft ass tone wasn't putting fear in any ones heart. I hated a man with no spine.

"Really Kyona, you got a nigga in the house wit my kids. I thought Xay was joking when he called me. As a matter of fact let me holla at you in the other room. Tell your poodle have a seat or something." He grabbed my arm not even waiting on me to respond. As soon as we made it to the hallway he shoved me in the downstairs bathroom and locked the door behind him. "So you won't fuck with me but you over here with bitch boy telling my son he bout to hang out with him. I expected better from you." He paced the small room like a caged animal and I could feel my skin crawl.

"Chrome get the fuck out of my house. You roll up in here after a year and act like you running shit. I told you I didn't want you the other day and I meant it. Yea I have a man. What did you expect? You all mad about a nigga around Xayden and for what? I know you like him but he isn't even your kid." He moved closer to me until I felt my back hit the sink. "What are you doing," I managed to get out before he pinned my arms behind me and kissed my lips.

His hard body enveloped mine and all I heard was my heart beating in my ears. I knew I should push him away but I couldn't. I felt my panties get wet and suddenly my arms were around his neck pulling him closer. I didn't give a fuck that Tyler probably had his ear pressed to the door. I just wanted to feel Chrome.

Just when I knew I couldn't stop he did, he stepped back, his eyes cloudy as they bore into mine. "You don't want me huh. It's all good ma I don't want yo ass either. Now go make sure my kids, both my fucking kids are ready to go. They can come home after your company leaves." He flung open the door letting it slam against the wall with a loud "bang" causing Tyler to jump back. Just like I thought he was standing outside listening like a kid.

Slowly I walked out behind him to find Xayden holding his book bag and Serina's diaper bag. I guess he was past ready to leave. He looked up at me and smirked. I was about to whoop his little ass but the look on Chromes face told me to let it go or I would be getting my ass whooped.

Tyler was sitting at the kitchen table his face resting in his hands, pouting like a small child. I fought the urge to laugh as I went to put my baby in her snowsuit. Handing her to her father I wished for a moment I was going too. Chrome was like a drug habit, one I had to really fight to kick. "Don't have my kids around no bitches," I said with an attitude. Thinking of him and another girl had me hot as fuck. All I could think about was thot bot Shaquita touching my baby and my skin crawled.

"Oh you mean the way you got my kids around your bitch," he shot back before slamming the door in my face. Sighing I gave him the finger even though he couldn't see and went to finish cooking my food. Chrome wasn't about to have me stressed the fuck out.

Chrome

"Daddy I don't like mommies friend Tyler. He called me Ayden and he looks like a teacher at my school. I want you to move in and be mommy's boyfriend," Xayden said as he climbed into the back of my car and into his booster seat. I didn't know what to say, I was mad as fuck that shorty had that lame ass dude around my kids but I fucked up me and her. I didn't want to listen to logic even though I knew in reality she wasn't going to be single forever.

After the kids where settled in the whip I just stood outside for a minute to get my head right. I had to get my girl back. If shit stayed this way I would be murdering every nigga she thought she was about to be with. I just didn't know how to make Kyona give me another chance.

I didn't even know where to take my shorties because I aint have no kid shit at my crib, I barely had food there. I had only been back in town a few weeks. Deciding last minute to just take them to Chuck E Cheese I headed that way. Xay ran around like a crazy person once we got inside and Serina just watched me the whole time. I guess she was wondering who the fuck I was. Her eyes kept searching the place looking for her mother. I was going to keep them for at least a week just to let Ky know I wasn't playing with her ass, but baby girl was gonna need her mom. She already had me wrapped around her tiny fingers and I couldn't do her like that.

Finally Xay was tired out and had gotten a bag filled with toys. This little dude could play hard. Driving back to Kyona's house all the calm shit I had been thinking left my mind immediately when I saw the green smart car still parked out front. Grabbing the baby seat and bag I motioned for Xayden to come on. He was making faces and shit, but he would have to just suck it up this time. I had to come up with a plan.

Knocking, Kyona came to the door in a pair of little ass booty shorts and a crop top. She didn't say shit to me and I was glad because I was hot as fuck. I made my way inside and breathed a sigh of relief that mister fucking goofy still had on all his clothes. I would have murdered him in front of everyone had that not been the case.

"Son it's time for you to leave. My kids are ready to come home and shit. I will give you two a few minutes to say bye or whatever but when I come back down stairs you better not still be here." I took Xayden upstairs to get him ready for bed. I could hear Tyler asking Ky if she was going to let me talk to him that way. I laughed to myself, what the fuck she was gonna do, better yet what the fuck was he gonna do.

Kyona

"Tyler look I will call you later I need to handle this situation on my own and without you whining in my fucking ears." I walked him to the door hoping he would leave fast so Chrome didn't leave him stinking in my living room. Tyler's smooth brown skin became interrupted by a deep frown. I had never seen his face have any expression but happy or sad, anger was a new one.

He stood there half in the doorway and half out looking like he wanted to say something else. "Hello, earth to Tyler is there something else you need to say? You over here looking like it's some shit you want to suddenly get off your scrawny ass chest and as you can see I already got one nigga with a whole lot to say. So either talk up or move along." My day had been up and down seeing Chrome and then having him reject me did a number on my nerves so playing mommy to Tyler's hurt feelings was not something I was interested in.

"Kyona take care of what you have to take care of. Just make sure you don't play fucking games with me." His voice was suddenly cold and his gaze was distant like he was look-ing past me. Deciding to not even address his strange behav-ior I shut the door behind him and went to take care of my kids.

I took Serina into the bathroom off of my bedroom and washed her up putting her in a yellow and white sleeper. I was so tired I didn't even care that Chrome was somewhere wandering around in my house. Gently I let my head fall back onto the mound of pillows on my King size bed. Holding my baby close I hoped she would settle down but the way she continued to wiggle around let me know she was wide awake. Lifting my shirt, I gave her what she wanted and prayed breastfeeding would put her to sleep.

"Damn," Chrome muttered standing in the doorway watching me nurse Serina. He didn't come closer just leaned against the frame. I couldn't tell what he was thinking his face gave nothing away. I tried to pretend he wasn't there but it was hard with my pussy ready to jump off the bed and onto his dick. Chrome stayed there watching me until I felt my eyes close, and sleep claimed me.

Chapter 3

Elite

I sat staring at the plus sign on the pregnancy test in shock. I felt my tender breasts through my shirt and ran my hand over my flat stomach. Why was this happening, I faithfully took my birth control, never missing a day. Suddenly I was filled with dread thinking about how I felt after I had my son ZJ. I literally just got back to feeling like myself a few months ago and now I was about to go through this shit all over again.

The crying, the miserableness, the loneliness and the fear, the fear was the worst. I was terrified that something would happen to my kids all the time and all those feelings were for no reason. The doctors said it was Post-partum depression. To me it was hell and to Zir it had to be something much worse. My hand shook as I still held the test. I wanted to look again because I felt like my eyes were playing tricks but honestly I was scared so I just sat there, mute, stuck.

The doorknob to the bathroom began to turn and I panicked. I didn't want Zir or anyone to know about this baby yet. I breathed a sigh of relief that it was my mother and not my man. "Damn ma you don't know how to knock on the door it could have been anybody in here. I didn't even know you were in my house." I quickly wrapped the test in some toilet paper as I thought of places to stash it later on.

My mom stood there with her eyebrow raised and a slight smile. "I came because I needed a favor. But let's talk about your surprise first," she blurted out. I loved my mother,

I really did. Connie was a good mom she always worked and pushed me to get a good education. She never let me go hungry or go without and I respected that. But my mother had her ways, she was always searching for love and in that pursuit she had made a lot of bad decisions. She also had a tendency to become easily excited, think small puppy or kid in a candy store excited. Sometimes I felt like I was taking care of an adult child.

Pulling her inside I hurried and shut the door. "Mommy I don't want anyone to know about the test, especially Zir. I will talk to him after I see a doctor and find out if it's for real or not." She looked at me skeptically then grinned before nodding her head. "Now you needed to ask a favor what's up," I asked hoping it was for some money and not anything more complicated.

She sat on the edge of the sink and began ringing her hands. Oh yea this shit was going to be complicated. "Well you know that Shaquita and the kids have been staying with us since the accident at her house."

"If her kid knocking her shit down with a car is what you consider an 'accident' then yea I remember." Shit me and Zir had a good laugh about it. I swear if that girl hadn't caused problems for my bestie she would have been amusing to keep around. Her life was like a weekly sitcom.

"Well umm, yea that, so the gas company was digging on our street and damaged some pipes underground. This caused a small flood and the basement became filled with water, actually the whole street did. They had to turn off the water and power in order to fix all the damage they caused and we all need a place to stay. It would only be for a few days. We tried a hotel first I promise we did but there wasn't any rooms available this week due to the Jazz Fest being held at the arena."

I was shaking my head no before she could even get

halfway through her speech. No way, not on a fucking good day, which today was not, would I invite her and her kids to stay in my house.

"Mom come on now, I don't know who I would fuck up first, Shaquita or those damn sons of hers. Why don't she go and stay with her home girl Keisha? Birds of a feather flock together or hoe together whatever. Anyway this is not a place for her. Hell no. You and your boo are welcome here and Shakita of course. She has a car, I see it at work, her and the kids can camp out there. I will even throw her a hundred bucks for gas money so they won't freeze."

My mother began to cry and is if on cue a knock followed. "E you ok in there," Zir's concerned voice boomed through the door. I hated how he sounded, so unsure, almost on edge. It wasn't a casual how are you doing, not like back in the day. He wasn't asking if I wanted a back rub or some breakfast. It was him making sure I wasn't trying to slice my wrists or crying for the third day in a row for no reason at all. The man I loved treated me like a small child, hell a sickly small child. He no longer felt comfort around me, just stress. I shoved the pregnancy test under the sink fast as hell and opened the bathroom door.

"Zir I'm fine, it's mama who is having a moment," I said my voice laced with annoyance. I walked out of the room leaving my mother to swim in her crocodile tears and think over the crazy request she brought to me. Just like I said a large fucking child and today I had my own children to attend to. "She thought that her, her man and his loose cannon ass family was coming to stay here for a "few days" because of some emergency." I was laughing so hard tears were streaming down my face. I just couldn't with this shit, not today.

"Damn E that's your moms and shit, don't have her out here crying. If she needs a place to stay we can do that for her. I swear yo ass be around her acting selfish as fuck." He was looking down at me like I had lost my mind. Shrugging I really didn't give a fuck if he thought I was selfish or not. I had to live with my mother and her captain save a bum ass nigga and his family my whole life. I deserved to be selfish when it came to my family and myself so him saying that wasn't changing how I felt.

"Naw Zir maybe you didn't understand what the fuck I just said. She wants Shaquita and her spawns of Satan to stay here with us for a few days. You know the boys who ran a car into her house? I see you over there looking all soft and shit because of my mother's fake ass tears but I personally am not moved. I need you to keep in the front of your mind that we have our own children who need to be kept safe."

"Elite Marie her kids are not that bad. You just have an attitude with her because of her and Kyona's situation," my mom said shaking her head. She was talking to me like a child who was having a tantrum over a toy. Funny when she was the one acting out.

"Ma it's cool for two days because that's what my man said. That's it though, if this shit aint wrapped up by Friday ya'll gonna be sleeping in the car with Shaquita and her critters," I warned.

"Don't worry about Elite I know how to fix her attitude," I heard him say as I walked away. I wanted to argue this shit with him and I knew if I did I would win but thoughts of the secret I was hiding from my husband had me deciding to let it go.

Before I got to the top of the stairs I figured I would make a few things clear. "Mom I'm not a fan of this bullshit, after this little "family" sleep over make sure you keep Shaquita as far away from me as possible. Whatever my reasons are for not liking her or wanting her around is none of your business. Also let her know if her sons even do so much as dream about being bad I will be there with my belt whooping they asses." Rushing downstairs I sighed as I suddenly felt the tears I prayed wouldn't come. Here we go with the hormonal rollercoaster.

Zir

I watched Elite walk away and I knew something was wrong. I also knew it was more than this shit with her mom and her people coming here. I only overruled her because I hated seeing moms cry like that. I lost my mom when I was ten so her mom and my aunt were all I really had. I stalked her ass downstairs and watched her stand in front of the window just staring. Tears where running down her face and as much as I was tired of this sad shit I would never turn my back on E. She was my everything and I didn't give a fuck if she cried for ten years I would be there to wipe every one of those tears.

Sliding my arms around her I held her close to my chest. We didn't even need words between us to speak, our bond was that strong. "Shorty what's wrong," I turned her around so she was facing me? I was happy this wasn't that mindless crying she did when she first had ZJ. This shit had some real feeling behind it. But at the same time I needed to know what the fuck was up. "Who got you crying," I asked but she didn't respond? Just buried her face in my chest and cried harder. I forced her to look at me.

"You mad about the stuff with your moms," I said wondering if maybe I pushed too far. She shook her head no and looked down at her pink manicured toes. "Someone did something to you," I tried to remain as calm as possible when I asked that shit because I felt my hand automatically going towards my nine.

"I'm good I just have a lot on my mind," she said softly. I knew her ass was lying. I been with Elite since she was sixteen years old. I knew her ass like a priest knew the Bible. "Zir you know I love you right," she said before her soft lips pressed against mine. Normally I would be trying to slide up in her wet pussy but for now I just wanted to show her love.

"Aight babe, you know when you ready to tell me what's really going on I'm here. I got you." I pulled her closer and ran my hand over her hair. "Yo I gotta make some runs I will be back later." I let her go and I swear it felt like I was holding my wife for the last time. Looking at my business phone I was annoyed seeing 'her' number flash across the screen again and again. If E ever found out about this shit I wouldn't be walking straight anymore.

I decided to ignore Alexcia for the moment and just go to the trap. I felt guilty as fuck with all that I had going on. When Alexcia and Isabella still lived in Florida this was much easier. I honestly didn't even think about them or the fact that I had a child my wife didn't know about. I sent a check every month and that was all. I had only seen Isabella in real life twice. It wasn't that I didn't care about her. I did, she was my flesh and blood but I had a family and honestly I loved them more. Her being without a pops in her life was on her scheming ass momma.

Seeing Chrome's truck outside I started to just leave. He aint know shit about Alexcia, and I had no intention on telling him. I came here because I wanted some peace and quiet. Somehow I knew my cousin was going to fuck that up. Pulling my hood over my head I walked up the leaning ass steps and used my key to get in. "This nigga right here, I see Elite finally let your ass come outside," he said with a joking tone.

Ignoring his dumb comment, I went to the back and started weighing the coke that my lil nigga Gauge picked up for me the night before. He drove trucks for a living and picking up dope was his number one delivery. My shit would be riding pretty next to the boxed goods for the local Wal-Mart.

Once I finished taking inventory I sorted out the batches to go to each customer so my runners could get on

TINA MARIE

that. I wanted to move some of the weight myself, but I knew I had to take my ass in the house tonight. Especially tonight, since I agreed to let the monkey from the zoo stay for a few days. I had to make sure my wife wasn't going to end up on an episode of Snapped. I wandered back in the living room just to see this nigga Chrome pacing the floor and looking at his phone. "What the fuck is wrong wit you?" I asked.

"Son you know Kyona dating that fucking Internet freak from back in the day? She told me she wouldn't give me another chance then I find out about this shit. I swear I want to put a bullet in this fool, but that shit is really on her. She gonna cause that niggas death and then what?" I could tell he was pissed the way he was sneering all the words he was saying. I never thought I would see crazy ass Chrome in love but that nigga was gone over Kyona.

"Cuz all I can say is go get your girl. You aint even got to kill ole boy just go there and show her you the man she needs. Don't let up, I know she is the one for you because you out here like a mad man."

He finally stopped walking around like a caged animal and sat on the couch. Before I had a chance to find any encouraging words my phone began vibrating nonstop. "Yo, what the fuck you want," I answered with heat in my tone. I was getting sick of this bitch and fast.

"Really Blaise this is how the fuck you talk to the mother of your child," Alexcia's annoying ass voice boomed through the phone as she used my government name. Clenching my jaw I hoped she would get to the point and fast.

"Man save the rah-rah bullshit and just get to the fucking point. Since you on my jack wasting my time let me ask you something, when the hell are you going back to Florida? Having you in my town doesn't work for me."

"Back to Florida huh," she said dragging her words out

26

like she was talking to a slow child. "Well since you live here and we have a daughter together I no longer live in Florida I now live in NY. So that part of the discussion is over. As a matter of fact, I should be asking when you will be coming to live with Isabella and me? She deserves a full time father as much as any other kids you got out here roaming around. Anyway I called to see what time we were having dinner together tonight. I feel like having sea food, unless you want something else."

I swear this hoe was going to make me choke the shit out of her. It was like everything I said to her went in one ear and out the other. "Hey yo, I never said shit about no fucking dinner. I'm done doing business for the day I have some family shit to take care of so I will hit you when I can." I hoped she just went with it because Chrome was looking at me like he was trying to figure out what was going on.

"Business, now we are business," she was screaming into the phone damn near bursting my ear drum. "Oh, we will be having dinner tonight or me and your wife will be having a conversation, so make it work. Now speak to your daughter before you go. Isabella come and talk to your no-good ass father," she instructed our daughter. I had to think quick because I had no intentions on getting to know a kid whose life I wasn't going to be a part of. Shit was all fucked up now and I wish I would have killed this bitch years ago.

"Naw tell her right now isn't a good time," I said before straight hanging up in her face. To be honest I didn't even know if Isabella was my kid. I slipped up once with Alexcia's ass and slid in her raw. Then bam nine months later she was crying baby. I just tried to quiet her ass down with money so it didn't get back to Elite. I used to be on a lot of bullshit back in the day but one thing I made sure to do was try and not let any of the dirt get back to E. Now it looked like my past was catching up to me.

"I got to get out of here I will holla at you later," I dapped up my cousin and got the hell out of there before he could ask any questions I wasn't answering.

Chapter 4

Keisha

I was so happy to have a day off since I had been working overtime the past few weeks. I wanted to take my kids to an indoor water park for their February break and I had finally saved enough PTO days to make the trip happen. "What are we going to do today?" I asked even though all Ju could do was drool and say "mama" and "dada". He smiled and did just that as he threw his cheerios at me. "Let's go see Daddy Ju," Cadence said before shoving her eggs in her mouth.

"Cadence, remember we talked about this? You can't call Ju daddy, and you cannot let your daddy know about him. It would hurt daddy's feelings." I never meant for shit to get so out of control in my life. It was always that way with me though always a bunch of secrets that led to drama and usually ended with me getting hurt. My babies face got sad and she pushed her plate of food away.

Before I could try and make her feel better a Face time call popped up on my phone. *Speak of the devil.* "Hello," I answered as Julian's face appeared on the screen. His lopsided smile showed his grill and the one dimple he had on his left cheek. He was the definition of sexy, milk chocolate and a tatted body to die for. He had a head full of waves but always had some kind of a hat on. Today it was a white Yankees fitted.

"What's up lil mama, what my babies doing," he asked? I turned the phone so he could see his son in the high chair. I sat back as he talked to Ju and Cadence. She wasn't sad anymore she was jumping around the table and singing some song. I tried not to watch Ju the whole time because he made my heart beat fast and my pussy wet. "Yo Keish come see me ma." He said as I turned the phone back to me. I figured Cease would be gone for a while since he had just left so I could get away.

"Alright, were you want us to come see you at?" I asked.

"Just come to my crib so I can spend time with the kids before I head out of town." I was happy to go see him, but sad he wasn't thinking about my ass, just the kids.

"Ok cool. Give me an hour so I can get them dressed." I hung up and grabbed baby Ju. "Come on Cadence lets go get dressed." I gave both kids a quick bath and laid out their clothes. I didn't know what to wear since it was cold as hell outside. If it was summer I could throw on some little dress and show all my goodies, maybe remind Julian of what I had to offer.

I settled on a pair of ripped blue jeans, a blue V-neck sweater and a pair of tan riding boots. I put Cadence on some white jeans and a pink and purple striped sweater from Polo. She had purple Timbs so she would be matching. I dressed Ju in blue jeans and a blue and yellow Polo shirt it was short sleeved so I put a long sleeved white shirt under. It took me three times to shove his feet in a pair of blue Jordan's because he kept curling his toes but finally all three of us were ready.

By the time I got us all in my all black seven series BMW my ass was sweating. As I began to drive I smiled at the smooth ride. I still remember trying to explain how I could afford this car to Ceaser when in reality Julian bought it for me. I didn't even have a job then, I had to make up all kinds of lies. I got my grandmother to cover my ass and say she was making the payments.

It worked in my favor for two reasons, one I didn't have

to explain the money and two it kept Cease ass from trying to drive my shit. Julian had made it clear he was never to be in my shit. The car was just another lie to pile on the rest. I swear I had so much bullshit going on I couldn't even sleep at night. I was so afraid that the house of deceit I had built would fall down around me.

I had a plan though. I didn't want to be labeled as another Shaquita, just because my mom was a crack head, and my dad was ghost my whole life. My kids would have better. I had been saving money for two years and made sure my credit was cleaned up. I wasn't just taking my kids on a vacation, we were moving as soon as we got home. March the first was the magic date. I got a two-bedroom townhouse in a suburb named Gates. It was quiet and close to my job. I hated that the kids had to keep sharing a room but the place had a bonus room downstairs that was going to be for their toys. I was going to do what I had to so we could move forward in life and not backwards.

I hadn't told anyone I was moving, not Ju or Cease. Shit I wasn't sure if I was allowing Ceaser's ass to come with me. Our relationship was past dead and not just because of my bed of lies. He had more secrets than me and I was no longer interested in trying to figure them out. There was a lot I could put up with, the put downs and different women, I could handle. But the fact he treated his kids like an afterthought didn't work for me. Ju had Julian, but Cadence was stuck with Ceaser's ass, and he barely looked her way.

Pulling into the driveway I looked in the mirror and smiled at my babies. They were both fast asleep, Cadence with her thumb in her mouth and her head hanging over the side of her booster seat. The door opened startling me out of my thoughts. "I got Cadence just grab him," Julian said as he picked her up like she weighed nothing. I wasn't arguing, shit when I had to carry her I felt like my whole body was going to give out. I wanted to shake lil Ju awake and make him walk but I decided against it and lugged him to the door.

Laying the kids down on Julian's bed I put the pillows around them and covered them up. Sitting on the edge of the bed I watched while he methodically walked around his room and began putting clothes into a black duffel bag. He barely looked my way. I wondered what the hell his problem was. We usually got along even though he was the one who broke my heart I never let that shit affect how I treated him. We had a kid to think about and even though Julian wasn't that hands on he was a good dad. I understood why he was the way he was, shit I had known him for over ten years. He wasn't like everyone else. His profession meant he needed to be focused and his attitude was not the best. Let's just say Ju wasn't a people person.

He zipped the bag and walked over to stand in front of me. I was only five feet three, so he towered above my head. I had to lean back to look up at him. "So, shorty what's good," he asked with a look I couldn't read on his face. I shrugged and waved my hand at the kids. Shit he asked me there for them and then gave me an attitude, so it was whatever. "Yea I see you done put my kids to sleep. What the fuck you do drug them? If I find out you gonna be walking with a limp." He was dead ass serious too.

"Hell nah I aint drug them, the car always puts them to sleep. They will be up in a minute running all over, tearing shit up." I looked around at his packed bag and felt bad that they had fallen asleep. "I'm sorry I know you wanted to see them and I'm sure you're in a rush," I said, my tone softer than before.

"It's cool I'm never too busy for them. Speaking of the kids when you telling bitch ass Ceaser that Ju is mine? I don't want him around my son and save the sad song about Cadence needing a father because you know I got her."

I looked down at my fingers because how the fuck was I going to tell my man of seven years his son wasn't his son. Ceaser may have been a bitch in the streets but he was still a nigga and stronger than me. He was most likely going to kill me and if he didn't hurt me and he left me than what? I would be alone.

"Look Julian I will when the time is right. Yea Cadence has you and Ju has you but when Ceaser leaves me who the fuck I got?" I asked with tears in my eyes. I didn't want Cease but the nigga I wanted wasn't fucking with me, so I had to settle.

Ju backed up with a dark look in his eyes. He slowly shook his head like he was having a conversation with himself. "Yea shorty I got you. I understand what you saying," he said his voice colder than ice. He walked off into his closet and stayed in there for a few minutes. My heart was racing because I really expected his crazy ass to walk out with a gun and dead my shit.

Instead, he walked out with stacks of money. He threw them on the bed next to me causing my ass to flinch. "Now you don't need that nigga so you have one week to tell him what's up or I will. In the future you can drop my kids the fuck off and pick them up when they are ready. Matter of fact, you can go wait in the fucking car." He turned his back dismissing me.

I got up and started putting my baby's shoes on, I wasn't doing this shit with Julian today. He was trying to play me like I was some random in the streets but he had me fucked up. "Come on Cadence, wake up baby we bought to go." I shook my daughter lightly so she could wake up, there was no way I could carry both kids. I damn near dropped Ju when I felt his hand squeezing my wrist with force.

"What the fuck you think you doing? I gotta wait until your bitch ass man not around for you to bring my kids over

and you think you about to just roll out. Oh, you got an attitude, what you need more money," he asked with disgust in
his voice?

"I don't want shit from you. I never asked for any
money that was all in your head. When Ceaser leaves I won't
have anybody to love me, not take care of me. I can take care
of myself, hell I been doing it. But I deserve to have somebody,
I deserve love. So just because yo ass don't want me and can't
love me, don't ruin all I have."

"So, yea we are leaving because you got shit twisted.
I'm not your other baby mother. Your money doesn't move
me your heart does." I fixed the cover over my son again and
swiped the tears that were crawling down my face. Snatching
my arm from his, I headed for the door. "Just call me when
you're done visiting the kids."

He didn't deserve my tears, none of these niggas did.

Shaquita

Getting rid of Julian without him seeing his daughter
was only a real possibility because I had police in my house.
Well what was left of my house. He warned me he would be
back and I knew I had to figure out something and fast so he
didn't realize Shakita was living with my dad.

I thought I would be staying somewhere for a few days
maybe a week until the landlord had the place fixed up. I
wasn't expecting her to straight put me out. She did it with a
big ass smile on her face to, like she wanted to evict me a long
time ago. I wasn't worried about it though. I found a cheap
place around the corner and had already done all the necessary paperwork for my worker to get me a rent voucher.

Staying with my dad and Miss Connie was a dream
come true. She cooked and they both helped with the kids.
I had babysitters whenever I wanted and free home cooked
meals. This bitch was living the life. Ray Ray must have felt

the same way because he had been behaving. Only Boobie was getting on every ones nerves, but that was the norm.

Now, thanks to some whack ass city worker the dream had quickly come to an end. Today was the day we had to start staying with stuck up ass Elite and sexy ass Zir. On one hand I was glad to be in his presence but on the other I didn't want to stay with light skin Barbie. Parking my raggedy car in front of their big ass house I felt out of place already. I knew I wasn't wanted here but I had nowhere else to go.

Boobie rode with me because he always tried to argue with his siblings in the car and my daddy threatened to leave him on the side of the road. Turning around I wanted to punch his ass already. He had his shoe strings out of his brand-new sneakers and was knotting them together with a gleam in his eyes. He was up to no good and we hadn't even stepped one foot in the damn house.

"Look Boobie let me fucking tell you something and this is some on the real shit. You better be on your best behavior in these peoples house or you will be sleeping under a bridge with the rest of the homeless little boys and girls." I wasn't lying either, I was going to be under the fucking bridge right along with him.

He stared at me, his eyes glazed over. "Mom, you aint about shit so don't threaten me. As soon as you find the next man to entertain and lose interest in us, you won't even remember what you just said." He unbuckled his seat belt and hopped out of the car, his shoelaces trailing behind him. I could ask why a million times but I was starting to think that Boobie was my karma for all the things that I had done in my lifetime.

Grabbing the suitcases, I drug them to the front door and waited on Miss Connie to get out of my dad's truck. I wasn't rolling up in Elites shit alone. Since I been working at her job I saw how she got down and it wasn't pretty. She was ruthless and wouldn't just fight a bitch she would break her.

"Come on baby, make yourself at home." Miss Connie said opening the front door and waiting on me to walk in behind her. I had been here before but never upstairs. As I made my way to the staircase Elite appeared out of nowhere.

"Naw slow yo ass down. Aint no making yourself at home in my shit. If anything, do the fucking opposite. Your room is on the main floor." Her face was balled up like she wanted to say something else. Even with a screw face she was pretty as hell. If I was into chicks I would have turned her ass out. Her long hair was flat ironed today and flowed down her back. She didn't have anything special on just some red tight fitting sweat pants with white and black writing and a matching cropped hoodie. "Well follow me don't just stand there like a lost puppy," she said with an attitude.

I followed her past the guest bathroom and down the hallway to a door I didn't even know was there. She flung it open to reveal a large bedroom with a mahogany bedroom set. The king size bed looked like it came from a hotel and there was a fifty-inch flat screen on the wall. Suddenly she stopped and looked behind me. "Uh you are missing a child, you need to keep those children with you at all times. If you move they move."

I turned around to see Ray Ray leaning against the wall and Boobie nowhere in sight. *Fuck.* Elite stood in the doorway blocking me from entering the room. Spinning on my heels I went to find my bad ass son.

Once I found him with his hands in the cookie jar in the kitchen. I grabbed him by his neck and drug him back down the hall. I swear it was like raising an animal. At least Shakita would be here to help. Speaking of my oldest she had wandered her ass away somewhere too. "SHAKITA," I yelled. I figured I might as well round up both kids before I made my way back into Elites presence. Shakita came running from

God knows where. "Get your ass in this room," I demanded pointing towards the room I was assigned. I felt like I was in prison. "Where are your bags?" I asked annoyed at her already.

Honestly she worked my nerves more than either one of the boys. But I did miss her being a babysitter, and her daddy paid the best.

"Her bags are where they always go when she comes over, so lower your fucking voice. She will not be in this room with the terror two and their misfit mother. Shakita you can go back upstairs and play baby," Elite said reaching down to hug my daughter. Shakita wrapped her arms around her like she was the one who pushed her pea head ass out of her cooch.

See I couldn't do it, I wanted to slap the piss out of her. Who the fuck was she to tell my kid what to do or act like they were friends? I bit the inside of my cheek to try and keep it together. If she wanted to fuck with me I would find a way to get at her ass. She had no idea the shit I be doing to ruin mother-fuckers lives.

"There are towels and wash cloths in the bathroom on the right. You know where the kitchen is and since this is only for a few days you shouldn't need anything else. If you do find your father and ask him because I don't want to be bothered." She flipped her hair, rolled her eyes and slammed the door behind her.

"Bitch," I said quiet enough so she didn't hear. Boobie looked at me with a smirk on his face. I had already had enough of this place to last me a lifetime. Grabbing the Advil PM out of my purse I motioned for the boys to come and take their medicine so I could go and catch a break.

*****

I read the look on my pops face that he didn't want me to leave the kids and go out. It had to be because we were in her house, but I didn't really care. My pops was the one who couldn't find a hotel so that wasn't my problem. I reassured him I wouldn't be out late because I had work in the morning. Even though I didn't give a fuck about giving him an explanation. I didn't want to waste any time going back and forth on the issue.

The work thing was the truth, I really couldn't be late anymore because I was on a final warning. I needed that job to buy furniture for my new spot. Getting in my car I tried to call EJ again but he sent me straight to voicemail. I didn't get my period yet this month so he better enjoy his little vacation from me while he could because he was next on the baby daddy team.

Driving towards Keisha's house I decided to see if she wanted to go to the bar and get some drinks. She was the only friend I had left. Over the years me and females never really got along. They always wanted what I had, even Keisha but I'm sure the beating I gave her fixed that.

I blew at her baby dad as he rode by me and I smiled. Ceaser was out for the evening so I knew she would be down to do something. She could always get the girl next door to babysit and I was even willing to pay this time. Shit her kids were well behaved so she had options. Knocking on the door she opened it and folded her arms across her breast.

"Yes," she asked? I could tell by the way her body was stiff and her face half frowned she hadn't gotten over our fight. I wanted to roll my eyes, but instead I forced a smile on my face.

"Shit why you looking at me like I'm your enemy or something. I was coming to see if you wanted to go to Gem and have some drinks. I'm staying with Elite, long story, but that bitch got me needing some shots." Her eyes bucked and she began to laugh. "What's so funny? I got you on a sitter so you don't even have to worry about that," I said hoping she said yes. Having no one to talk to sucked, I needed my friend.

"Girl you out here smoking that shit or something," she said. Her voice sounded amused. I looked down at what I had on, red skinny jeans and a black leather jacket. My black ankle boots and plain silver studs weren't over the top. I looked perfect for a night at the bar.

"You beat me with a bat, while my back was turned and then you drop by asking me to go out. Are you fucking crazy, did rats eat your brains. Bitch I would rather go out with my crack head ass mama before I went somewhere with you. Now you need to leave because my kids dad is about to bring them home."

She slammed the door in my face and I swear I felt like crying. I never gave a fuck about having a bunch of female friends in the past, but that was because I always had Keisha in my corner.

Without her I had no one, my mom was still on Jay and Broad selling her old ass pussy for a dime bag of coke. I had no female cousins or even aunts who would speak to me. I had fucked most of their men or scammed them at some point. I knew Elite's ass would never really treat me like a sister even once our parents got married. Sitting in the car I began scrolling my phone trying to find someone to call. I missed Chrome's crazy ass. He was never really for me but came to fuck on the regular. He was the closest thing to a boyfriend I ever had.

Turning the key I began to slowly pull away until I noticed a familiar black Range Rover pull in front of Keisha's house. Cadence hopped out of the back and a tall guy climbed out of the front. Wait was that tall guy Julian....

Chapter 5

Kyona

I woke up in the middle of the night after having a dream that Chrome was in bed holding me. Seeing him today must have had my head fucked up. My senses too, because I swore I smelled his cologne. Letting my eyes slide to the clock on the cable box I started to panic when I saw it was four in the morning. What the fuck. Serina never slept that long without me having to feed her.

Jumping up I looked in the crib to check on my baby and felt my heart drop at the empty space where she should have been. Running out of the room I slammed into a hard body as soon as I hit the doorway. "Arghhh," I yelled as I tried to kick the unknown figure.

"Hey girl hush all that shit before you wake my kids up," Chrome said holding me by my arms, so I didn't drop. I could see the laughter on his face. I guess from me trying to fight him. If I wasn't still trying to figure out what was going on I would have laughed at my weak ass hits too.

"What the hell are you doing here?" I demanded still in shock. I didn't know rather I was excited he was creeping in my room in the middle of the night or pissed. Looking down I could see my stiff nipples through my thin white tee as I felt my pussy get wet. Well I guess excited.

He followed my gaze and let me go. Stepping back he looked like he was using all the self-control he had in him to not reach out and touch me. "Ma you wish I was coming in here for yo ass. I was coming to grab a blanket for baby girl.

Like I said before, I don't want you," He walked around me and went to grab the pink blanket from the end of the crib.

I could feel my face get hot. I was embarrassed and my feelings were kind of hurt. Even though I had no intentions of giving him another chance I still wanted him to want me. I guess you could say I was confused. Well I would take the good night's sleep if I couldn't get anything else. Taking care of a baby all alone was tiring.

*****

It had been one week since Chrome had figured out where I lived, and I swear he was in my crib every day. Any time Tyler was supposed to come over he was there, when I woke up his ass was there. He would just be sitting on my couch calm as fuck, always claiming to be spending time with his kids. Half the time they were asleep or doing something else. I hoped he found his way to his own shit today because I had a headache out of this world and was just not in the mood.

I was assigned a new class at work and it was the same bullshit as always. I swear I was teaching at a clown college instead of a business. "Miss Kyona can you go over the call center greeting one more time for me," one of the new girls named Jayda asked.

She was one of those low-key ratchet chicks. She knew enough to dress appropriately for work. She had on a khaki pencil skirt and a white button-down shirt. Her nude heels accentuated her long legs and she even had on a pair of glasses, I guess to touch up the professional look. But I could see it in her eyes, she was as hood as they came and some way, some-how I knew she was going to be a pain in my ass.

Finally I was able to clock out and head to my car. If I had to answer another dumb ass question I was going to turn into a work place killer. Pulling up to the daycare I got the kids together as fast as I could. "Xay mommy isn't feeling well so its Popeye's for dinner tonight," I said and he began clapping and shouting "yay". He loved the chicken from there.

By the time I made it home I could barely hold my head up from the pain. Happy my driveway was empty I fed the kids and took two Excedrin praying something would take the migraine away. Tyler had called a few times but I sent his ass right to voicemail. Elite was also ringing my phone but talking to anyone was out of the question right now.

As soon as Serina was washed up and had her snack of breast milk she drifted off to sleep. Seven o'clock and I had peace and quiet. I let Xayden watch a movie on his iPad in my room until he fell asleep, or I did. "Damn were my food at Ky, you couldn't get a nigga even a two piece and a biscuit," Chromes voice said waking me out of a deep sleep. Here we go. Rolling my eyes I regretted it after I felt the pain hit me hard. "Yo what's wrong with you," he asked leaning over me and putting his big ass hand on my forehead.

"I have a headache and your hand isn't helping things or this bright ass light. Chrome this shit, you popping up when you feel like it, somehow getting in my house while I'm asleep. It doesn't work for me. I wake up you in my kitchen or watching my TV. I go to bed and you are wandering around the house like you're my man. You're not my man, Tyler is and you always being here doesn't work."

He got this crazy look on his face all of the sudden and I decided to try and explain this shit another way. "You can calm down because you look like you about to have a heart attack. I'm not trying to keep you away from the kids. All I'm saying is let's work something out. A schedule so you can pick them up, or I can drop them off. I'm just trying to get my life back."

He sat on the edge of the bed and dropped his hands in

his face. "Look shorty you got that. We can talk about this shit tomorrow when you feeling up to it. I got the kids tonight just rest up and shit," he said. I swore his voice sounded sad but I couldn't be sure. He took the kids to bed one by one and suddenly I was alone.

Chrome

Shit I didn't know what the fuck I was doing here every day. I knew I could have just worked out some shit to pick up my kids but I craved being in Kyona's presence. I didn't want Tyler around not because of Xay and Serina but because I didn't want to think about a nigga touching my girl or fucking my girl. So I made sure I was here every night when she got off of work.

I was using Xayden's iPad to message him so he could let me in and shit. Hell that was how I found out where she lived, location services was on point. I barely found time to fuck the new pussy in my life, her name was Jayda and she was a straight freak. One of those hoes that lets you bust in any hole, fucking her was like a kid taking a trip to an amusement park, nothing but fun and a sticky mess.

Watching Serina sleep I still couldn't believe I had a shorty. I knew she was mine even though Kyona offered me a blood test. I didn't need that shit. I was taking to her my mom this weekend because I didn't even tell her she was a grandmother yet. I knew she was going to be hurt and when she finds out about how I treated Kyona I was going to hear her mouth. I waited all this time because I just wasn't ready for all of that.

Throwing Jayda a text telling her to be ready for me in the morning I stretched out next to Xay and tried to get some sleep. Instead I found myself staring into the darkness. I couldn't relax, I needed Kyona. After a few hours I just said fuck it and got out of the bed. Making my way back into her room I watched her body slowly rise and fall as she slept.

Her ass was falling out of her purple panties and she had her legs wrapped around a pillow. My dick was bricked up and I couldn't deny how much I wanted her anymore.

Lowering my body on the bed next to her I didn't waste any time. I snatched the pillow and threw it on the floor with an attitude, like it had did something to me. Ky rolled onto her back and her legs fell to the side. I could see how wet she was by the stain on her silk panties. Sliding my finger in her honey pot she moaned and moved her hips pulling me in.

I wanted to take my time with her body since it had been a while but fuck it. Pulling the scrap of purple to the side I released my dick from my boxers and plunged right in. Kyona's eyes flew open, and I just knew she was going to fight me, but instead her soft hands ran over my back. The feeling caused a chill to run through my body.

Ripping her thin shirt in half I slowly licked the sensitive area around each of her nipples and watched her arch her body. Tangling my hands in her thick hair I gently pulled remembering her head hurt. Her exposed neck was so delicate, so sexy to me I couldn't help but to plant kisses there. It sent her over the edge, and she began clenching her muscles as she came.

She squealed as I bit down on the spot that I just kissed. The feeling of her was one I missed, shit I craved it like a crack head with his next hit. She was my addiction, no amount of freaky sex could compare to how she felt. This was home. This was love.

Kyona's eyes rolled in the back of her head once another orgasm took over her body and then she went limp. "Naw baby girl you aint done yet, come take this dick," I demanded as I rolled her on top of me. She began riding me cautiously. She couldn't handle my shit anymore and that made me smile. Either she wasn't fucking Tyler or his dick was little as hell. Whichever one it was, the thought caused me to smirk.

Slapping her on the ass hard as hell I grabbed her and made her feel all this dick. "Chrome," she said calling out my name. I knew I wasn't going to make it much longer. Kyona had me under a spell. She spun around and started popping her pussy. Watching her ass bounce up and down and the thick juices from her cumming back-to-back did something to a nigga.

Before she could react I pushed her off me and onto her knees. I was going to give her ass one of those punishment fucks, she deserved it. "Owww," she cried out as I went in deeper. Her little cries weren't stopping me.

"Don't run Ky, I know you want this dick." With every stroke I thought about how she wanted to move on from me and I wasn't going to let her. Before I knew what was happening my hand had crept around her neck and I was lightly choking her. I guess it turned her on because she started throwing her pussy back on me. I could feel my knees getting weak as I bust a big nut deep off inside of her. She tried to jump off the dick but I held her closer. "Don't move, you gonna give me another kid," I said feeling my eyes close.

Chapter 6

Shaquita

Hopping out of the car so fast I hit my knee on the steering wheel I limped back to Keisha's house. Julian saw me as I approached but he didn't even look fazed. That shit made my blood boil. He pulled Keisha's son out of the back and held him close. That was when I saw it, how could I have missed this shit in the past. Baby Ju looked just like Julian's ass, same dimple and thick eyebrows. I guess Ju stood for Julian, I never asked the lil nigga real name. Shit I barely remembered my own kids.

"Cadence go inside baby," Keisha said as she stepped onto the porch. I could see by the look on her face she knew what was up. Another ass whooping was headed her way.

I didn't give a fuck whose kids were watching I was tapping that ass again, only this time I wasn't stopping until she was dead. "Bitch you had a baby by my man," I slapped the taste out of her mouth as she pushed her daughter inside. Before I knew what had happened she punched me so hard I flew down the front stairs. Getting up I went to hit her again but was met with more blows to the head. Shit she was hitting hard as hell, I felt dizzy and tasted blood. I knew she could scrap but I didn't think she could match me. Why was she even mad, she fucked my people?

"Shaquita fuck you, I don't feel bad for nothing I have done. You knew I was in love with Julian but he had to be a part of your fucking plan. All these niggas out here with money who don't want kids and you trap the one who I wanted for my man. I don't regret shit except being friends with your trifling ass for so long. I wonder if Julian knows that Shakita doesn't even live with you anymore," she yelled into the night air, and I felt my body shiver.

I got up and started to back away towards my car. It seemed like I was moving in slow motion. I watched Julian hand Keisha their son and check her over with concern. He said something in her ear that I couldn't hear before kissing her and sending her inside. Wow. He treated me like I had aids but he was out here wifing this bitch when she had a whole man of her own.

The truth was besides Ray Ray's dad who was just gross I wouldn't have minded settling down with my kid's fathers, if they would have been into me. Deciding now was not the time to reminisce on the many ways I made a fool of myself for Julian I turned around ready to make a run for it.

I just couldn't help myself I had to address the situation before I walked away. Turning and facing him I made sure he saw how angry I was. I had the most twisted, ghetto girl, bitter baby mama look on my face. "Of all the bitches in the world, you had to pick my best friend. I should fuck you up. You make me beg and work for any bit of affection you ever gave me but you over there pawing all over that hoe. There aint shit different where me and her are concerned. We are both some crack babies who be out here in these streets doing whatever to survive."

"So, what the fuck makes that bitch so special," I yelled. I saw the curtain move and I knew she was watching us. Thinking back to the night I beat her with a bat and left her on the ground in the snow I smiled. I would be coming for her again.

I knew she loved Julian. But hell what girl in our neighborhood didn't. We never really loved a nigga, just his money or what he could do for us. How was I supposed to know her ass had real feelings? He moved a few feet closer to me but I didn't bother to move back.

"So what if I have a baby with Lakeisha. Why is it your fucking business? Do yo ass even know where my child is? You out here looking like you got a date on hoe row, drunk and high but you mad at Keisha?" He pushed his hands in the pockets of his Versace jeans and I could tell he was trying not to strangle me.

"Fuck you Julian. What you gonna do when Ceaser come catch you with his woman and fuck you up?" I didn't care anymore, I was wishing Cease pulled up right now and shot his ass between the eyes. I knew I never had a chance with him and I could guarantee that I wasn't getting any more money now. Julian had become useless in my book. He laughed when I said something about Ceaser fucking him up. Julian's ass was so cocky. Waving my hand I turned to walk towards my truck. I didn't have any more time to waste on him.

"Click, Click," I heard as I felt cold steal press against the side of my neck. I didn't know why I ever fucked with Julian, I knew what he was into long before I had Shakita. His occupation had nothing to do with drugs and everything to do with murder.

Rumor had it when we were kids that he sliced up his parents then set them on fire. I do remember his house burning to the ground with them in it but the news just said it was an electric fire. The gun dug into my skin as he applied pressure and I felt hot piss trickle down my leg.

"Don't say a fucking word, just get in the truck and don't try no funny shit or your face will be on the front page of the morning paper." I walked to the truck just knowing that this was it for me. He was about to take me to some wooded area and leave my body for the animals. In high-school my teacher said bears ate her sunflowers. He was going to feed me to those same bears. They would find my shoes, maybe my watch.

Shit my dad would probably think I ran off to go and have fun because that was the kind of shit I used to do. Ok real shit, that was the kind of stuff I still would do. We sat there in silence Julian still had the gun pointed at me and no expression on his face. "I'm waiting on you to tell me where my kid is at. Or we can sit here until I get tired of looking at you and blow your fucking brains out."

"246 Wayland Lane," I said my voice shaky with fear. I didn't even have time to mourn the loss of the money he provided me with. I should have left without saying anything else. Had I not approached Keisha about him, maybe this wouldn't have happened. I was too busy mentally picturing my funeral, the one no one would come too except my father and his girl. He pulled off and drove with one hand on the steering wheel. We pulled up in front of Elite's house and he gave me a strange look.

"Yea you fucking the homie Zir too, yo ass really got some kind of death wish. I was going to kill you but shit imma just let Elite get that ass." Julian laughed as he walked around to the driver's side and snatched me out by my arm. I swear I heard something pop the way he was grabbing on me.

I took out my phone and called my dad so he could open the door. I was happy it was only nine at night and not too late. I didn't know that Julian knew Zir but I guess it made since. The Roc wasn't that big of a city and killers and drug dealers usually hung in the same circles.

The door flew open catching me off guard. I could see the disapproving look on my father's face as he stood there. "Dad, this is Julian. He is Shakita's father, and he has come to get her for a visit," I said as an introduction. I looked back to see somehow Julian had put his gun away and replaced the look of rage to one of calm just that fast.

"Well as you know Shaquita I have custody of Shakita at this point so she won't be going with just anyone. Where has this so-called father been all this time while you have been mistreating her," he asked eyebrows raised? I could feel chill bumps from the cold look of hate in Julian's eyes. He had no idea I wasn't treating Shakita well.

Shakita ran down the stairs and jumped into her father's arms like she was up there being tortured. "Daddy, I missed you so much and my brother. I want to go see him and show him all my new toys my auntie Elite bought me and my grandpa and grandma. Maybe you can take us all to Sky Zone, Me, Ju and Cadence. Then miss Keisha could cook us tacos," my daughter went on and on letting me know that any spare time she spent with her father was also in the company of his other child.

I felt my blood simmer under my skin and if it wasn't for the fact that I knew he had that gun and didn't care about using it I would have talked a lot of shit. Maybe even put hands on his ass. She looked over Ju's shoulder and I swear her little ass was smirking once she noticed me standing there.

"It's nice to meet you Julian. I thought these children didn't even have a daddy that's why we took Shakita in, me and my fiancée Connie that is. Plus, we had been helping Shaquita financially of course, so this is a shock to me. I can see you have a loving relationship with my granddaughter this is the happiest I have seen her, ever. We will be happy to sign over custody of Shakita to you if you want to take her of course. I just ask that you allow us to see her sometimes we do love her and under no circumstances should she be returned to her mother." My pops was standing there looking relieved. I guess the thought of raising a kid at his age was stressful.

"Baby girl go get your stuff from upstairs while I talk

to your grandpa," Julian instructed Shakita and she of course ran off to do what he asked. "Sir I think you and your daughter need to be having a different conversation. She has been playing more than me and only God knows who else, a word of advice I wouldn't financially help her anymore.

She was getting twenty-five hundred dollars a month for Shakita plus extra for holidays, birthdays and school clothes. Shit my other baby mom was getting less than that for two kids and she made sure our daughter was in private school. Has clothes, toys and other necessities. You really need to do something about your child before someone hurts her one day."

"Now as for my shorty, she was coming with me no matter what. I appreciate your help but I got this from here. I will leave you with my contact information so we can set up some sort of visitation." He leaned against the wall and waited patiently for Shakita to come downstairs. The front door opened and Zir walked in on what had to look like some bullshit happening in his front hall.

"My nigga what's good," he greeted Julian and then slid his eyes my way. "Damn son this you?" he asked with laughter in his tone. Shit I was every-ones joke today. I crossed my arms with an attitude.

I had never heard Julian laugh a second in his life until now. Only this was like those laughs that serial killers had, the crazy ones that they use when being walked down death row. "Hell nah, this was a mistake I made six years ago that I'm still paying for. I thought she was you, I was preparing ways to tell my daughter that Elite had killed her mama."

"Son you know better than that. I don't even get down with loose ass broads like that. I can see the resemblance now, Shakita looks just like your ass. Come on in and make yourself at home while you waiting. You want a drink," Zir asked him as they left me standing in the hallway like a stranger?

Facing my dad all I saw was disappointment in his eyes before he turned and walked away.

Lakeisha

Finally the kids settled down, both of them in my bed because all the commotion caused by Shaquita's ratchet ass had my kids wound up. I tried to not argue around them or no shit like that so seeing me fight someone was new. Even though I know it didn't seem like it, I was trying to give my kids a stable life. At least one more stable than mine was growing up.

I couldn't help but think about the way Julian was just acting all concerned about me. I wished it was genuine, but I'm sure it was just because the kids were there. We been beefing since he demanded I had to tell Ceaser about Ju not being his. I only had two days left and honestly I didn't know what I was going to do. Julian was a man of his word, so I knew he would fuck me up and tell my secret.

I got up and went downstairs to the bar, the whole time my heart was beating fast as hell. I really fucked up this time and I didn't see a way out. Fixing a cranberry and Vodka I enjoyed the burn as the Grey Goose flowed through my system. I climbed back in the bed and leaned my head back. Closing my eyes, the alcohol started to take effect and I started to relax.

As soon as I heard the downstairs door open I felt my shoulders slump and my body tense up. I wasn't in the mood to deal with Ceaser. I was hoping he would stay out for the night, hell a few nights. It was something he would do all the time, but I guess tonight luck just wasn't on my side.

"What the fuck your ass in here doing," he asked eyeing me suspiciously as he walked in the bedroom. He stripped throwing his clothes all over the floor. I held in any comments I wanted to make. I had a slick ass mouth and keeping quiet was not my specialty. I hated that he was such a slob, one of the many things I couldn't stand about this nigga.

Picking up my cup I took a long drink telling myself in a few more weeks I wouldn't ever have to see his face again. Rather I would be lonely or not, I had made a decision over the past few days. I was leaving Ceaser behind once I moved. We al deserved a better man in our lives and if we couldn't find one, I was cool rasining my kids alone.

Last week I took a day off and I went through all of our clothes and junk we had. I threw away and donated anything we didn't wear, fit or use. All the kid's clothes and toys were in plastic tubs ready to be moved out. I knew Ceaser wouldn't notice because he never went in their room. I was only bringing our bedroom sets. The other furniture would be replaced.

Ceaser got on the bed and damn near smothered Julian so I hurried and snatched him out of the way. "Why you always got these kids in the fucking bed. I know they asses got they own shit," he barked talking shit as usual.

"This my fucking bed and if my kids want to sleep in the bed with me then they can. If you don't like it go sleep somewhere else, like somewhere you pay some fucking bills." I made sure to give him the, *I don't give a fuck face* before I moved Cadence closer to me and lay back against the pillows.

Moving Cadence must have startled her awake because she shot up out of her sleep and started crying. Trying to hold her and rub her back I almost shit myself when she started crying for her daddy. I knew this was going to end badly. "I want my daddy," she screamed causing Ceaser to look at her and reach out his arms. "No I want my daddy Ju," she said as she fought Ceaser off. Her screams got louder as her little arms and legs were flailing all over.

Shit, shit, shit. Once her tiny fist hit him in the face Cease pushed her back and got off the bed which caused me to jump up. I wanted to run, but where the fuck was I going with my kids sitting there. I played out every scenario on ways for me to grab them and get out fast but nothing I thought of seemed realistic. This was why I didn't want to tell Ceaser this shit. I wondered if Ju ever thought what this nigga was going to do to me. "Cadence, who the fuck is Daddy Ju," he asked while walking towards me with murder in his eyes.

Cadence sat on the bed sniffling. Hearing Ceaser's tone caused her to stop screaming and look up. She was too young to really understand the mistake she had made. "He is Julian's dad. Well he said he is my daddy too. He buys me clothes and shoes and takes me to get ice cream and toys," she said in a sleepy voice. I crossed my arms because I knew it was about to be some shit so all I could do was try not to show him I was afraid.

Before I could blink this nigga had his hand around my neck as he slammed my head into the wall behind me, "Who the fuck is Julian's father," he asked? His voice was even, real calm like those crazy people you see on crime TV. I couldn't even think because now both kids were awake now and crying. "Is Julian my son," he seethed in my ear?

Shaking my head no, I didn't let a tear fall. I wasn't ashamed of my son's father one bit. I loved Julian. Cheating on Cease didn't mean shit to me because he had been dogging me out for years. I didn't have enough fingers and toes to count the times I told him I was lonely. The times I begged for his attention. Or asked him to stop fucking randoms.

He let me go and began pacing the room. I didn't waste a second standing there I made my way to my kids and held them both close. I just wished he would leave and go cool down somewhere. "Wow you really fucking cheated on me," he said as he walked from the window to the dresser and back. It appeared he was talking to himself instead of asking me any questions, so I didn't bother with a response. "WHO IS HE?" Ceasar boomed from across the room? This time I knew he wanted me to answer.

"Ju from over the East," I responded with an attitude. No point in lying now. I guess Ju would be happy, he got what he wanted. No more hiding his only son, he could get him whenever he wanted. I knew me and Ceaser were done and I felt partly relieved and partly saddened. I had been with him for so long it felt like I was losing something that I needed, something familiar. He wasn't the best boyfriend but he was mine and now it would just be me. It made me wonder if I would have ever moved and left him behind. Was I really at the point that I couldn't or wouldn't take any more from him or was I just talking a good game?

Fighting the urge to apologize or beg him to not leave me I shifted on the bed to lay baby Ju down. He had fallen back asleep, must be nice to not have a clue about what was going on around you. Cadence was rubbing her eyes and sniffling into my side. "Yo you a real dirty bitch," Cease said as he ran up on me and gave me a fist to the head. Jumping up I went to hit him back but was interrupted by the sound of gun shots and breaking glass from the front of my house.

"What the fuck," I yelled. My heart racing, I snatched my kids off the bed fast as hell and ran to the bathroom in the middle of the house. There were no windows there and it was the safest place I could think of at the moment.

See shit like this was why I had to move from over this part of town. This was the first random shooting on my street but I'm sure it wouldn't be the last. Thank God I had my kids in bed with me because all the shots came through their room which was in the front of the house. Shaking I realized that Ceaser's ass wasn't in the bathroom with me. "Nigga you come to my crib with this shit for real son," I heard him yell before I heard more shots. Only this time they seemed like they were coming from inside my house.

"Hey Ceaser pay us the money you owe or next time we won't miss," I heard someone yell before the sound of tires screeching. After that was the sound of the front door slamming and another car pulling off. Then everything was silent, the kids sat huddled in the tub in shock just watching me. Their bright eyes wide and shining with tears broke my heart. I didn't know what to do so I just sat there for a while praying the gunmen were truly gone.

I don't know how long I sat there holding my kids, shaking and crying. I must have fallen asleep because my head shot up when I heard someone on the stairs. Looking around for something to protect us with I heard someone calling my name. There was footsteps going from every room upstairs and headed my way. "Keisha, were the fuck you at ma," Ju's voice said coming from outside the bathroom door.

"Ju," I cried out softly. My throat was raw and scratchy from all the crying I had been doing. He burst through the door his gun out in front of him. I was so relieved I started crying all over again. "Ju you came for us," I said. I thought he was out of town so him being here was like a dream. Maybe I was dreaming, shit maybe I got shot and I was dead. Having Ju save me seemed like something that would happen after I had died.

When he grabbed me out of the tub and my back hit the spigot causing me to yell out in pain I knew my ass was alive. "Ma you hurt," Ju said running his hands over my body inspecting me. Noticing the scrape I just got, he must have been satisfied I would be ok.

"My kids better fucking be straight," he snapped pulling them into his arms. I just knew he was somehow going to blame me for this, but instead he snatched me back close to him. I swore for a minute he was thanking God but I may have misheard his low tone.

"Come on and get what you need you not staying here," he commanded. "Oh and I don't give a fuck about your punk ass nigga. Where the fuck he at anyway," he said a look of disgust on his face.

I didn't waste time grabbing some duffel bags and pulling clothes out of the already half packed house. "I told him about Ju being yours. We were arguing when the gun shots started. He owed some dudes money and this was just a warning, at least that's what they said. He ran out of the house and left us after I ran in the bathroom with the kids to hide."

He clenched his fists but didn't say a word just grabbed the stuff I had put together and carried it outside. I slowly followed. Seeing all the bullet holes in my couches, TV and picture frames in the living room had me breaking down all over again. "Mama don't cry, daddy is here now it will be ok," Cadence said placing her hand in mine.

"My baby is smart, daddy got ya'll so don't worry," Ju said walking up to me. "Keisha, I got you shorty so wipe those tears. I will have someone come and get all your stuff and put it in storage until you can get a new place." Julian leaned over and kissed me, it was intense like he was putting all of his emotions into it. I could feel his heart beating through his hoodie and in that moment nothing else around me even mattered. Not my fucked up situation, or what I was going to do next. All that mattered was me, him and my kids, together.

Chapter 7

Elite

Waking up I rolled over and realized Zir wasn't next to me. Lately he had been acting strange. Staying out all night, ignoring a lot of phone calls, everything from the cheater's handbook. I knew the drill, me and him had been there before. But I couldn't tell if it was me hiding my pregnancy making me paranoid or if he was really up to something.

Me and Zir didn't always have an easy relationship. When he was straight trapping, long before he became a boss he cheated on me, a lot. It wasn't until I packed my shit and left that he straightened up. He never put any bitch before me, but I was tired of fighting those smuts every day. I would have women approaching me at school, the hair shop hell even the grocery store. He wasn't fucking all of them but because he was such a whore they all thought they had a chance.

I didn't want to get out of bed, already this baby had me fucked up. But since it was a secret, I had to act normal. Forcing myself into the bathroom to brush my teeth and wash my face I slid my feet into a pair of pink fluffy slippers and went to get my kids up. Lala was in her room playing with that big ass doll house Chrome bought her for Christmas. Shakita was in there too. Lala liked having another girl to play with so we had convinced Ju to let her stay the weekend so he could get shit together on his end. "You guys want breakfast," I asked?

"Yes can we have pancakes mommy. Please," Lala asked

dragging out her please. I shook my head yes and went to get my baby up. I guess I could stop calling him a baby since he was going to be two years old soon. ZJ was still in his crib knocked out with his butt in the air. I swear he was like his father. Stayed up late and slept all morning.

Walking in the kitchen I was so happy to see my mom had already cooked breakfast and was setting the table. At least something good had come of my mom and her people staying here. She was cooking, cleaning and running behind the kids.

"Good morning baby," she sang out while kissing me on the cheek. I sat on the stool at the island waiting for a plate of something to come my way. The smell of bacon had me ready to tear some shit up. Seeing the red velvet pancakes with whipped cream my mom set in front of me had my ass grinning. As soon as I took the first bite I heard the front door open.

Zir walked his ass in like he wasn't just getting home at eight in the fucking morning. Just like that my appetite vanished. "Morning ma," he said hugging her and snatching a piece of bacon. "What's up?" he asked turning my way. I looked right through his ass like he wasn't even talking to me. Fuck him. I wasn't about to play these games with him. I had enough shit going on. Picking up my phone I began scrolling through Instagram liking every nigga I saw. I was mad and I lived for petty shit.

Suddenly I felt my phone being snatched out of my hand. "Yo what the fuck you doing? I know you heard me speak to your spoiled ass. You can't respond?" I didn't even bother trying to get my phone back I got up making sure the stool flew backwards and hit his ass. "E, what is your problem ma," he said. His face held a confused look. I don't know what the fuck he was confused about.

"You nigga, you're the fucking problem. You forget

where you lived last night? Or you just didn't care enough to come home. Shit at least back in the day you tried to hide your dirt. I guess now you don't even care about me that much." I wanted to punch him in his face but honestly, he was just too fucking tall so I settled for kicking him. I knew it hurt because he cursed under his breath.

"Damn that's why he be cheating on yo ass, you stay talking to him crazy. Zir if you were my man, I would be on my knees ready to welcome you home no matter what time of the day." Shaquita licked her lips at her last statement. See this was the shit I was talking about. Him and my mother thought trash like this was ok to bring into our home. Hell Zir wasn't my fucking playmate or baby daddy he was my husband.

"Shaquita, shut the fuck up. Don't address my wife moving forward or finding a place to sleep will be the least of your problems." He grabbed me by the arm and pulled me close. "As for you, take your ass upstairs so we can discuss your problems in private," he hissed in my ear. I stomped up every stair like a small child and I didn't give a fuck. I wanted Zir to act right and Shaquita to get hit by a bus and die. I had enough of everyone today. Zir followed right on my heels and I knew he wasn't in the mood for my attitude today.

As soon as we made it to our room he closed the door and locked it. He walked up on me until the back of my knees hit the bed and I fell backwards. "You know a nigga in these streets getting it so you can live good. Why you making all that noise and shit? What you wanna come sit in the trap wit me all night," he asked a serious look on his face. He was on top of me now and I could feel his dick poking my bare thigh. He thought he was going to distract me with sex. I mean yea that shit usually worked but not right now.

"Aight cool. What time you want me ready tonight," I asked while trying to slide out from under him? I used to sit on the block with him when he was still selling dime bags so I had no problem with being by his side no matter what business he was handling.

"Girl ready for what? You think you bout to hang in the fucking trap house? Get the hell on with that shit, and just know once I'm done tearing that pussy up you bout to go unlike all those niggas pictures. If you don't, I'm running up in each one's house and blowing their brains out."

Feeling his lips on mine my pussy betrayed me, and it felt like I was flooding the bed. He pulled up my shirt and started playing with my breasts. They were sensitive because of my situation and I couldn't help the moans that were slipping out of my mouth. Feeling him yank my little shorts off I didn't waste no time playing in my pussy. Zir damn near jumped out his clothes then sat back and watched me.

"Girl you so fucking sexy," he commented as he stroked his man. I took my finger and trailed it up my body until it rested on my lips. Sticking my tongue out I began licking all my juices. I knew that shit was fucking with his ass because the smirk he had on his face fell away and he was just gazing at me with pure lust. See Shaquita aint have a damn idea what I did with my nigga. I turned around and gave him that perfect arch, the one that kept him going crazy. I gasped when he slid all ten inches of his thick shaft inside of me. He didn't even take his time so I knew this was going to be some rough sex.

Even with him pounding into me and slapping my ass like I stole something I managed to cum back to back. "Slow down babe," I whined trying to scoot up a little and give my girl a break. He deaded that shit and pulled my hair forcing me to be stuck in one place. His lips on my neck went from gentle kisses to straight up biting and I knew he was almost there. Since I was already fucked up I decided to pop my pussy on his dick and give him something to think about all day.

"Fuck, Elite this pussy gets better every time. If you ever give my shit away I will kill you," he growled in my ear as he sank as deep as he could and released all his seeds inside of me. Normally I would have been fussing about him not pulling out but it was too late for that now so I just enjoyed the feeling. Pulling me into his arms I didn't fight him. Shit my ass was as weak as a newborn baby.

"E, you gotta just trust me ma. I don't want anyone but you. You got a nigga heart. Shit you got my last name." The last thing I remember before I went back to sleep was feeling him kissing me on the forehead.

Waking up alone for the second time today put me in a worse mood than before. He straight left me here with a sore pussy, all alone again. "Stupid mother fucker," I said out loud to the empty room. Suddenly I saw something brown jump at me from the other side of the bed. "Argh," I screamed as I flipped the blanket over the squirrel and jumped out of the bed. My legs were tangled in the sheets so I ended up falling to the floor struggling to get up and out of my room. Not caring that I only had on my lace thong I ran outside and slammed the door.

I felt the small body the minute I spun around, damn I was moving so fast I hit one of the kids. Looking down I was filled with so much rage I had to step back and remember this was only a child. There sat Boobie on the floor, he was laughing so hard he had tears streaming down his cheeks. It didn't take me long to realize that he was the reason a wild animal was running loose in my room.

"You little motherfucker," I shouted grabbing him by his ear. All thoughts of him only being a child were left. I opened the linen closet in the hallway and snatched the belt that I kept there to scare Lala and Xay when they were acting up.

"No, you can't hit me you're not my mama," he cried out. His tears of laughter turned to tears of pain as I went to swinging. I was catching his little ass all over. Arms, legs anything that was showing skin. He was trying his hardest to get away but I had a death grip on his arm.

"I can hit your ass because this my fucking house. If you not gonna act right you get your ass beat." I beat him until my arm was tired. He stood up and stumbled as he went towards the stairs. "Hell nah, where you going?" I turned him towards my room and shoved his ass inside. "Get that fucking animal out of my room and if anything is damaged your punk ass mama is paying for it."

Looking up my mother was standing at the top of the stairs with her mouth wide open. Shaquita was behind her slow dragging up the steps like she was drunk or high already. I mean damn it was barely noon. I wonder if that bitch was popping pills or something. Probably. "What is the problem and why was my son screaming," she had the nerve to ask like she gave a fuck.

I leaned up against the wall waiting on him to evacuate the squirrel from my room. The closer Shaquita got the angrier I became. Before I could think abut it I was flicking the belt in her direction catching her bare legs.

"Oh my God, Elite what the hell is wrong with you," my mother screeched.

I glared at her, "you can be next if you don't leave me alone." Her and Shaquita stood there staring at me, slightly in shock. A few minutes later he came out dragging the creature by its tail. I stood and watched as he threw it outside and closed the door.

"Shaquita this is the first and last warning about you and your kids. Stay the fuck out of my way or you will be next to get thrown out by your tail and the streets will be your home. This isn't juvenile hall or a homeless shelter I don't have to keep ya'll." I made sure to slam my bedroom door as I went in to clean up whatever mess her kid made in my there.

I felt so much better after whooping the shit out of Boobies little hood ass. I knew I really hurt him because I was letting go of all my frustration and anger. Shit I had even forgotten about the baby growing inside of me at the moment. Sitting on the freshly made bed I turned on the TV and tried to rest my mind. I really thought I was good, but after ZJ fell asleep for his nap I found myself having a full-blown panic attack.

For a while I just sat there fighting for every breath until I decided to call him. He answered on the first ring just like I knew he would. "I need to see you," I choked out. He told me to meet him at the Applebee's near the mall. Throwing a red and gold Pink hoodie on with black tights I slid my feet into some gold sparkly UGGS and grabbed my oversized Louie bag.

"Elite where you going? Every time I come home you running the fuck out. What's up?" Zir stood in the doorway looking like a black God. His dreads were pulled back in a ponytail and I could tell he had just got his beard trimmed. He had just enough facial hair to be considered a part of the beard gang but not enough to be labeled a terrorist.

I could feel my hands shake. He didn't know about Paul even after me seeing him for months and I had no plan to tell him. There was a time I couldn't make it through the day without Paul. He had become a lot of the things Zir used to be. Until the streets became his best friend and that is why Paul became my confidant. And the reality was someone else had probably become his.

"You just going to stand there," he asked? His eyes were cold, I had never saw Zir look at me like that before. Not when I told him I hated him after I had Lala or when I burned up some special addition Bulls Jersey after he flirted with the jogging ass neighbor down the street. I was losing my man because of this disease, this depression. Or was it because of this baby. I had to let him go, not because I wanted to test his love but because I didn't want to keep hurting the man I truly loved. This thing I was going through was out of my control and that was what was the most fucked up part.

I cancelled the meeting with Paul since I actually felt better once I made the decision to leave Zir, he deserved to be free. He deserved better than a woman who was emotionally broken. Erasing my messages I decided to take a hot shower. The steam in the bathroom relaxed me and I almost felt back to myself as I dried off and put on some body oil. I needed to feel Zir one last time before I said goodbye so I put on some sexy lingerie and made sure I fell asleep on top of the covers. I wanted my fat pussy to be the first thing he saw when he walked in the bedroom.

I felt his presence before he got on the bed, he stood there in the moonlight watching me. I wondered what he was thinking, was he mad or sad. Was there another bitch on his mind? I didn't want to hurt Zir, he was my everything. And that was why it was time to let him go.

I closed my eyes thinking about the day we met. Zir saved my life when some neighborhood gangs decided to have a gun fight in front of the corner store. He shoved me behind him and took a bullet in his arm. Bloody and all he threw me over his shoulder and carried me up the street and out of the way.

"My knight in shining,-" I started to say to the fine ass boy that rescued me as he set me on my feet.

"Naw ma, don't say that corny shit. It was some right place right time situation. I aint nobodies knight in shining nothing. I be out here doing the same shit they be on. You need to be more aware of your surroundings before you end up just another pretty face on the news."

I smiled up at him and let my hand rest on his chest. My heart felt like it was going to beat out of my body. Maybe it was the adrenaline from almost being shot but I swear it was being in his presence. I knew at that moment I loved him. "What the fuck you looking at me like that for. I'm a grown ass man and you a little girl. You got me over here feeling like a creep or some shit." I looked down and noticed his dick print through his grey sweat pants.

It took a while for Zir to really give in to me. I would stalk the same block I almost died on trying to bump into him every day. And once I did I made sure to show out. I was wearing the shortest shorts, tightest jeans and shirts that had all my titties out. It wasn't until the day I was ready to just say fuck it and give up on Zir, that I finally got his attention.

I stood outside the store sucking on a blow pop and flipping my twenty inch sew in over my shoulder. "What's good ma," this sexy little light skin dude said walking in my space. "You gonna let me lick on you like you licking that candy," he said. He ran his hand down my cheek and smiled. I wasn't really feeling him but since Zir wouldn't give me any play I decided he could be something to do.

"Yea, you gonna do that for me baby," I cooed as I licked my lips.

"Yo King, this me," Zir said as he walked our way. King shook his head and held up his hand as an apology before he stepped off. "What the fuck you doing out here ma," he demanded as he invaded my space. He gently pushed me further against the brick of the building. He was so close I could smell the mouth wash he had used that morning.

"Go home. I don't need my girl out here distracting me while I'm trying to work." He kissed me then, his lips were surprisingly soft. I thought they would be rough like the rest of him. That was the start of me and Zir.

"What you thinking about," he said startling me? Feeling his long fingers caress the backs of my legs I almost forgot that I was lying on the bed in some little see through shit. "I know you not sleeping, I saw you with those eyebrows all scrunched together. You only do that when you're thinking. Elite is there something you need to tell me," he asked as he dropped down on the bed?

Shit I wanted to tell him everything that was in my heart right now, but I needed to be close to him one last time. "It wasn't about anything important. Come to bed, I want to feel you inside of me." I watched him lay back and close his eyes. I could see the worry lines and I knew he was stressed. Maybe he wasn't fucking around on me. Maybe he was having problems with his business. I should let him rest, he looked tired as fuck.

Suddenly his eyes popped open. "Shorty what you doing, I was expecting a show or something? I mean you got dressed up all sexy and shit. You just gonna watch me all night," he said talking junk.

He pulled me on top of him and slowly kissed me before flipping me onto my back. It was like he knew what I needed without me saying it. Instead of fucking, Zir made love to me. After kissing every inch of my body he slowly entered my honey pot. Feeling him fill me up for the last time brought tears to my eyes. The way he held me closer to him while slowly giving me long strokes was driving my heart, body and soul crazy. Suddenly he stopped ran his hands through my hair. "Elite, I love you," he said before he took my bottom lip in his.

"I love you too," I whispered.

His touch was driving me crazy and I began bucking beneath him. I could feel my tight pussy drawing him in, closer and closer to my womb. "Zir, I'm going to cum," I cried out as my pussy tightened around him. My orgasm caused him to nut deep inside of me. After he fell to the side of me he pulled me close. I didn't even care that he was sweating everywhere I just wanted to be in his arms this one last time.

Waking up I knew I wouldn't forget this Sunday. It was a day that would change my life. Rolling out of Zir's arms I said a little prayer asking God to help me through. "Blaise," I called his name low, a part of me hoping he wouldn't even hear me and I could do this another time.

"You calling me by my government and shit, what's really good," he asked sitting up and stretching? His eyes narrowed and I knew this wasn't going to be easy, not one bit.

"We need to talk," I said holding back tears.

Zir

Looking down at Elite I could feel my palms start to sweat. I knew some shit was up from last night. Shorty was fucking me like it would be the last time. She held on to a nigga the whole night like I was about to float away and now she wanted to talk. The first thing I could think was that Alexcia had gotten to her. I knew bitches didn't care about breaking up a man's happy home and lately my baby momma had become very unpredictable. I went back and forth in my mind trying to figure out if I should just start explaining this shit when she started to speak.

"Look you know I thought I had got past the post-partum depression shit but I don't think I have. I have spent the last few days really thinking about this. I don't want to take you through that again. Blaise you know I love you, there isn't anything I wouldn't do for you, so I am going to do this for you." She handed me the princess cut diamond ring she wore on her ring finger along with the wedding band.

"E, what the fuck you doing shorty?" I snatched her hand in mine and tried to put her rings back on but she was steady fighting me.

"Look, this aint no fucking joke. What I'm doing is leaving you. This shit is over. I don't want you to move out because our kids need both parents but you are free to do you. Please do you. I want you to be with a stable bitch. One you don't have to worry about all the time, someone stronger than me." I didn't even know how to react; this shit had a nigga stuck. Was she serious right now?

E jumped off the bed and backed away. See I didn't even give a fuck about her crying and shaking. Elite thought I was about to chase after her ass but not this time. Anger flowed through my body, a nigga been out here working double time trying to make sure nothing fucks up our marriage and she suddenly wants to end it. "This some bullshit, but it's cool." I threw the rings in her face as I made my exit.

"Blaise, where are you going," she asked, her voice all sad and shit? I almost turned around and went to her but fuck that.

"I'm about to go find me a strong bitch, like you said."

Chapter 8

Kyona

"Xay come on boy," I called out. I looked at Xayden who was still in the bed curled up like I didn't have a job to get to. Normally he was the first one up so I had no idea why he was still asleep. Maybe he snuck his iPad or video game in the bed last night. Shaking his little ass he half opened his eyes and rolled back over. Feeling his head he didn't have a fever so I shook him a little more. "Let's go," I said as I went to get the baby ready.

"Come on lil mama. You over here looking like your daddy and shit," I said getting baby girl ready for her day. She was smiling and drooling like I wasn't talking junk. Once she was in her pink Nike sweat suit and matching white and pink Roshe's I rubbed some leave in conditioner in her hair and did two fast ponytails. Looking at Serina was like looking into Chrome's face for real.

I still felt like having a baby with him was all a daydream and I would soon wake up and find out it wasn't true. I did love his ass, I just couldn't do stupid, and the shit he did to me was just that. Plus I was sure it was just the start of how ignorant he could be, I wasn't sticking around to see whats next.

"XAYDEN," I yelled as I made my way downstairs. His boots and book bag were still sitting in their spot so he wasn't ready and I was. Turning I huffed my way back to his room with an attitude. Xay was laid out on his bed with his clothes on. "Xay, you ok baby," I asked my attitude turning to concern? He slowly nodded his head and forced himself to get up. I felt his head one more time but he was still cool to the touch.

"Ok let's go, the bus will be here any second and don't forget you have karate today," I reminded him since he loves karate. But that barely got me a smile. I felt something deep in my belly twist, this felt so wrong. I knew my baby and this wasn't him. "You want me to have Chrome come watch you at Karate today?" At this point I was trying anything to get him to perk up. That was it, he smiled and shook his head yes. He walked downstairs and put on his stuff.

"Come get this fruit for breakfast," I said handing him the container of all his favorites. The school gave them cereal or bagels but my babies both loved fresh fruit and veggies and I made sure they got them. Watching Xay get on the bus I hopped in my car and made my way to the daycare. I would have preferred that the baby was watched at home but with my mom far away I didn't have anyone. I did like the fact I could log in on my phone and watch video of her all day and see what she was doing.

"Morning Miss teacher," Jayda called out to me when I walked in. I swear I couldn't put my finger on why I hated her ass but I just did. She was on time, somewhat professional and all of that but when I saw her face I just wanted to stab her eyes out with the number two pencil on my desk.

"Hey Jayda," I replied in a dry tone. The day went by faster than I thought it would. I kept checking my phone to see if Chrome responded to my message about going to Xay's Karate but nothing yet. He had been acting so petty since I fucked him and then brushed his ass off the other day. He would have Zir call about the kids so he didn't cuss me out- that's what he told his cousin. Cuss me out for what I was still trying to figure out.

Waiting on Elite slow ass I leaned up against the front

of the building. Today was warm for February, almost fifty-nine out so I didn't mind. "Bye Miss Teacher," Jayda called out as she sashayed out the door. I wanted to tell that bitch I had a name but even though I was clocked out I was still at work and trying to remain professional. She looked around kind of confused like she didn't know what to do next. I knew that bitch was slow. Seeing an all-white Range pull up I wondered whose dumb ass nigga she was fucking.

"You ready," E said walking up startling me.

"Yea, just watching this thot in my class. She got some-one man picking her up from work. I wonder if that nigga girl know where he at." I was laughing hard as a bitch until I saw the dumb nigga picking her up was my nigga. Well, my used to be nigga. Chrome walked around the back of the truck and greeted her with a hug and a kiss on the cheek.

Elite's face was turning red and I knew she was about to go off. But for once I was going to beat her too it. I didn't even waste words I just walked up to his ass and punched him in the side of his head. "Next time I text you about our kids an-swer the fucking phone. I won't even address the rest of this shit." I looked Jayda up and down as I said the last part.

"On no bitch, you are not going to put hands on my man. I'm about to whoop your ass, I don't care who you work for. He is the nigga in the streets, so I hope you know I don't even need this job." Jayda called herself running my way with her scrawny ass fists bunched up. I didn't even bother to look up, I wasn't moved, not one bit.

Just like I knew he would Chrome snatched her ass up and threw her to the ground before she even entered my space. "Naw baby girl I don't play those games. First off this my baby mom, only one a nigga ever gonna have so respect her or get fucked up. Second you need this job like a mother fucker I only pay one bitches bills and you looking at her." I rolled my eyes at the fact he called me a bitch but smirked at the sad ass look on Jayda's face.

"Now your son has karate at six, he wasn't having a great morning and wanted you to be there so check your fucking messages and make sure you're on time." I walked to the car not looking back. I knew Chrome was going to be there. He played games with me but not our kids.

"Wow he like the bitches that work here don't he," Elite said laughing as we made our way to her car. "Girl I don't even think I am going home. Ever since I told Zir we had to break up he has been a complete asshole. Then Shaquita and her constant drama. I can't wait for her ass to leave. I told my mama two days it's been a fucking week already."

"I don't know how you doing this shit. Her and her Bebe's kids would have been at the homeless shelter on Main St. or sleeping in a parking garage. I'm surprised the kids haven't leveled your house yet. As long as those gremlins don't touch my God kids, I guess they will be aight." I was serious too, I fight fucking kids.

"Look I whooped the shit out that little boy the other day, that fucker put a squirrel in my bed. I woke up and damn near pissed on myself." The look on my besties face told me how disturbed she was, but I couldn't stop laughing. Bent over and all I couldn't even breathe.

"Really Kyona Nishay, that was not funny. Imma drop his ass off at your house and then we will see whose laughing. Anyway bish keep Chrome out your bed because I may be using my key later on," she said giving me the finger before she climbed in her car.

Chrome

"Yo, are you coming or what I got shit to do?" I snapped at Jayda as she sat on the ground looking like a sad pound puppy. I went around to the passenger side of my truck to get in. If she didn't get up by the time I sat down, she would be taking a taxi or an Uber.

She slid in the passenger side with tears streaming down her face. "Yo shorty what you crying for, I know your feelings is more hurt than anything else." She sobbed some more and put on her seat belt. I didn't really care. I should be the fucking one crying. I didn't even realize this was the same job that Ky worked at, shit I never been out here before. This was a set-back to getting my girl in my arms where she belonged. It wasn't Jayda's fault but I wasn't about to let her go at my wifey, that was taking it too far.

"Chrome really, I didn't even know you had kids. You straight dissed me for that bouije ass Kyona. I hate looking at her every day in class and now I have to look in her face knowing you dissed me for her. I'm supposed to be the woman in your life right now. You didn't even have my back when I thought she would fire me for fucking wit her ex-man. You telling me you not giving me money if it comes down to it for real?" She was dead ass serious too, her gaze intent on mine and her hands folded tightly in her lap.

"Jayda I know you don't really know me. You are cool to kick it with, bend over the couch and fuck here and there but as for me spending my money on you. Hell nah. That's not me. I could lie and say that it's because my kids need my money more than some bitch but even before them I didn't spend on hoes. I mean you cute and all, got your own shit but I smashed on the first date. Where am I dropping you off at because I got shit to do." I made a point to look at my Rolex and let her know her time was short.

"Oh, I thought we would hang out or something," she licked her plump lips and made a pouty face. I mean yea her face was saying nut all over me, but no one came before my kids.

I just drove to her crib, if she needed to go somewhere else that was on her. I didn't even like hoes in my vehicles because of shit like this. Lil ma called me today asking for a ride since her car was in the shop. This was a one-time mistake and wouldn't happen again.

As I pulled up to her apartment building she sat there like she was waiting on something. "Ok you home and shit so bounce," I said looking at her with cold eyes. It was almost five and I wanted to shower before I went to see Xay.

"Zaddy you really not coming inside. Let me thank you for the ride," she said in a seductive tone. I felt like that damn emoji where the nigga hitting himself in the face. Was I speaking a foreign language? Stuttering? Hell, maybe baby girl was deaf, did my cum drip in her ear last time and she didn't clean that shit out?

"I know you heard my baby moms say my son has something he needs me to be at. Now get the fuck out," I reached across her and opened the door. She slowly climbed out and slammed my truck door. I started to run that bitch over but I didn't have time for that today. This was why I couldn't commit to these females. I didn't have the patience for their antics and I wasn't going to prison over any domestic shit.

Seeing my mom call me I knew I had to come clean and tell her I had a baby soon. I let this shit go too long now and the longer I waited the angrier she was going to be. Real talk I was only waiting since I didn't want her to know how bad I fucked up with Kyona. Deciding against going all the way home and fighting the rush hour traffic I stopped and grabbed some Chipotle and headed to the Dojo. I pulled up five minutes before and I noticed the car I copped Kyona parked in the lot.

Walking in I saw her on the left side of the room sitting on some wooden bench. I felt bad this was the first time I came to see my little man do his thing. I had to at the very least fix the communication issues between me and Ky. I wasn't about to be no dead-beat dad. "Move over ma," I told her as I went to sit down next to her.

"There is a whole bunch of places to sit over there," she pointed to the back of the room. I shoved her little ass until she slid down and grabbed Sierra from her.

"Hey daddy's girl," I said kissing her on her fat cheeks. She smiled and hit me in the mouth with her tiny hands. "Yea your momma taught you that didn't she?" I thought about how Kyona caught me in the head earlier. I swear my ears were ringing when she was done. If it was any other girl, she would have gotten hit right the fuck back.

I looked over at her and smiled, Ky was cute as fuck in her black joggers and grey cropped sweater. She had her hair up in a ponytail, nothing fancy but I could see all the men staring her up and down. Reaching out my hand I pulled her closer to me. I was gonna start bussin in this mafucka if these niggas aint stop watching my girl. Kyona glared at me but didn't make a scene.

Kyona

Feeling Chromes hand on me I got goosebumps. I wanted to hit him again for fucking with Jayda's simple ass but now wasn't the time. I sat back and watched Xayden go through his routine of kicks and punches. He seemed to be moving slower but was trying his best to perfect each movement. I knew he didn't want to mess up because Chrome was here watching him.

We all clapped as the kids ran up to this huge punching bag and performed jump kicks. When it was Xay's turn he jumped and suddenly fell back and hit the floor. His eyes rolled in the back of his head and he wasn't moving. Me and Chrome ran across the room at the same time.

"What the hell happened, did he hit his head or something?" he demanded looking like he was about to fuck up the teachers in the class. I knew something was wrong with my baby earlier but because he didn't have a fever, I brushed it off. I held his hand afraid to move his head until the ambulance came. I heard his instructor call one so I knew they would be coming any second.

I looked up at Chrome with fear in my eyes. I felt guilty and afraid all at once. Xay was rarely even sick so I didn't know how to take this. I didn't expect my six-year-old to collapse for no reason I could figure out. I should have done more when he was acting strange in the morning. I was just worried about getting to work on time.

"Don't worry he's gonna be aight. Come on ma you strong so just hold on. You know I won't let anything happen to my son." Chrome was saying all the right things but nothing felt right.

Chapter 9

Zir

"Zir give me your fucking phones, both of them. I know you been cheating on me. I can feel it in my heart." Elite stood in front of me shaking, her tears were flowing so fast that her shirt was soaking wet. Ever since our son was born, she had been acting crazy and that shit was wearing a nigga down.

I thought we had finally gotten past this, but she was right back to the same thing lately. Her telling me she wanted out of our marriage was the last fucking straw. I had enough to deal with between Alexcia and her bullshit and the streets. Even though money was good there was always police, snitches, and enemies to worry about. I just needed home to be my peace.

"E for real ma, you on that bullshit, you the one who told me to find a new bitch to fuck now you stressing me about what I'm doing, how sway." I threw the phones at her as I made my way to the shower.

I loved Elite but at this moment I didn't even want to look in her face. I wasn't no fucking baby and she wasn't about to run me. I took my time letting the hot water drip down my back and over my head. I wasn't fucking stupid though. I had Alexcia crazy ass blocked so I knew she wouldn't be calling or texting. I saved her name under the bank I used for a business loan. I washed up and stepped out to silence. With E that could mean anything, so I made sure to prepare myself before walking into the bedroom.

I was ready for some blows to the head, but the room was empty. My phones were on top of the all-white comforter still lit up. I laughed because she had cussed out some female customers in my business phone. She told Valencia she was going to rip out her eyes and feed them to the pigeon's downtown. I didn't give a fuck, these bitches rather business or whatever always knew my wife came first.

I went ahead and checked on the kids and found Elite curled up in bed with Lala. I covered them both up and kissed them on the cheek. I wanted to make E come back to bed but why fight with her especially with her family in our house. I didn't need any more chaos, a nigga was tired.

I grabbed a bottle of Henny and drank it to the head so my mind could get some rest. I hated sleeping without my wife so the liquor helped. I woke up to soft hands lightly running over my leg and making their way to my dick. "Fuck yea E, you come to make it up to zaddy," I said enjoying the feeling. She pulled my man out and got right to work. I guess my baby was feeling really bad because she hated giving head. I found myself moaning. "Yes Elite suck that dick girl," she was putting in work because I felt like a straight bitch the way she had me calling her name.

Suddenly the bedroom door burst open, and the bright ass hallway light was blinding me. "Nigga you want Elite to do what," my wife screeched standing in the doorway with murder in her eyes. What the fuck? I threw back the covers and damn near had a heart attack when I saw Shaquita with my dick in her mouth.

Before I could shove her ass off my shit Elite had already grabbed her by the back of her neck. I wanted to stop her because I aint want my wife in the middle of no fuck shit. Before I could jump up her mother was standing in the doorway her eyes bucked at my dick still being out. I hurried and threw the covers over myself.

Elite was beating Shaquita ass like she stole her money, but what could I say, shorty was wrong as fuck. She never even had a chance, her eyes were both swollen and blood was pouring from a few spots on her body. "Yo E, chill ma, you gonna kill her and shit," I called out after a while.

Elite looked up while choking her and gave me a look of death then calmly went back to what she was doing. Shaquita began fighting back since she couldn't breathe. Her legs were flying all over until she got a good kick in and knocked Elite back.

"Elite stop, just let her go before you hurt the baby," Miss Connie yelled causing E to drop Shaquita like she had the plague. I wondered for a few minutes was Shaquita's ratchet ass pregnant again until I saw Miss Connie rush over to Elite's side and start checking her over. Shaquita grinned and stood up like she had just found treasure. I knew then that Elite was the one pregnant.

"Yo Shaquita you try it and they gonna be cleaning your brains up off the floor." I showed her the gun I kept next to the bed as I pointed it her way. She drug her wounded ass out the room somewhere as I jumped out the bed and made my way to Elite. I didn't give a fuck if my dick was swinging for all to see this shit had to be addressed immediately.

"What the hell mom, I told you I didn't want anyone to know about this baby and you still open your fucking mouth. I wouldn't even be in here fighting this bitch if it wasn't for you and your loose pussy. Next time find a nigga whose kids have some sense." Elite was going in on her mom and Miss Connie opened her mouth to apologize but I knew it wasn't going to change a thing, so I stopped her.

"Hey Ma, just walk away. I need to speak to Elite about this shit." She looked at us and shook her head before making an exit. I knew her feelings were hurt but I agreed with my wife. She had to start thinking with her head and not her heart or whatever else she was using.

I was just as much at fault. I should have never let this bitch Shaquita stay in our house. I stood in front of Elite just waiting on shorty to give me some sort of explanation. "Say something, what the fuck. You over here hiding my baby and shit?"

"I wasn't hiding anything. I was going to tell you once I made a decision on what I was going to do. This was the shit I didn't, want or need, you stressing me over the situation." I had never put my hands-on Elite, not in all these years and through a lot of shit but I couldn't control myself. Did my wife just tell me she had to make a fucking decision on our baby?

My hands were on her hemming her up against the wall as I felt tears pool in my eyes. "Elite for real ma, you trying to decide if you want to what keep our kid?" I could see it in her eyes that I was right. The fact that she had even thought about killing my seed made me crazy.

"So, what's the problem, I don't take care of you or our kids? I don't fucking give ya'll everything? The whole fucking world is yours ma. I give you time, money whatever the fuck you want. I guess that shit aint good enough for you to have another baby wit a nigga. When you didn't know if Lala was mine or that sucka ass nigga Maze's did I turn my back on you?" I asked that shit even though it wasn't a question.

I was at every appointment, satisfied every craving and never once questioned if Lala was mine. I knew the moment she was born but even when I didn't know I never let that shit change how I treated E or our unborn. "Ma why the fuck you doing this shit to me?" I had always protected my heart but Elite was the only one with the power to break my shit and she was doing it now. She was my reason why, I hustled hard because she was at home waiting on me and after all that she was willing to betray me. To kill my child.

"You don't get it Blaise. I don't think I can do this again. It's about you and me and our kids. I'm scared as fuck, what happens when I have another baby and I go through the same shit I went through with ZJ. You are not thinking. You going to stick around watching me cry all day, who is going to take care of our kids when I can't because post-Partum got me down and out?"

I could see the fear in her eyes, and it tore me apart. What could I say to that? I didn't have to live that shit, not in her shoes. I was mad and hurt but I was also worried about Elite. Punching a hole in the wall above her head I turned around and left. I couldn't do this shit right now.

Elite

I cried myself to sleep that night after locking myself in my bedroom. If I saw Shaquita or my mother I knew I was going to prison for premeditated murder so it was for the best that I stayed to myself. I called in sick as soon as the clock hit six AM. I just couldn't function today. I called the only person I knew who wouldn't question me to come and take care of my kids, Chromes mom. As much as that nigga got on my nerves I swear his mom was my savior. She was the mom I wished I had. She came and got the kids with no questions asked. Just gave me a hug and a smile.

I heard my mom questioning her outside my bedroom door, but she handled it well. Not even engaging my mother in her bullshit, she told her she didn't have to explain any-thing to her about my kids and kept it moving. The rest of the day a few people knocked on my door but I didn't answer, I wasn't talking to anyone. I wanted my bestie with me but all of my calls to her went unanswered. By nighttime I was start-ing to get worried because we spoke every day.

Hearing Zir's voice downstairs caused my heart to race and my breathing to become labored. *Great another anxiety attack.* I hurried and texted Paul because I really needed someone to talk to. As soon as Zir walked in the bedroom I was already dressed in some tights and an oversized sweater. I ran in the bathroom to wash my face and brush my teeth. I didn't even brush my hair just threw on a white hat I had laying around. I felt like I was suffocating, and I needed to leave ASAP.

"We need to talk," he said making his way to me. I swear I almost fainted from the stress of being in his presence. The stress of the situations in this house and the baby I was carrying. Shaking my head no, I dodged him and ran all the way to my car. I sped the whole way to the Hyatt downtown praying I didn't get pulled over. I had a bunch of speeding tickets already because I didn't really pay attention to the speed limit.

Finally making it, I parked in the garage and took a few minutes to try and calm down. Paul wasn't my creep; he was a counselor I met through some program at my OBGYN. We were only supposed to talk during the times they provided us and for a few months. He ran a trial program but was such a help to me he agreed to meet me anytime.

"Hey," I said as I walked up to the table. Paul stood up and hugged me a little longer than I liked but I shrugged it off. Paul was cute if you liked bald headed guys. I didn't, his body was banging though. He had to work out at least six days a week.

"Damn girl I never saw you out here with a hat on. You must be stressed. Not that you aren't still beautiful." He grabbed my hand and smiled. I slowly pulled my hand away feeling uncomfortable. I hadn't seen Paul in person for a while since I had been feeling good so I wasn't sure were all this was coming from. He had never flirted with me in the past or maybe I just never noticed.

"Yea I have a lot going on. I found out I'm pregnant again and I honestly don't know what to do. I don't want to keep this baby and go through being depressed again. I don't want to put my family through that because it wasn't just about me. Now my husband's mad, I think we are going to end up getting a divorce because of this shit."

"Well, I told him we should get a divorce. It's not really what I want, but I know it's for the best. Either way I think it's too late, he hates me. I have never seen him so mad before." I covered my face with both hands and closed my eyes. I hoped something Paul said made me feel better. Or at least gave me the answer on what I should do.

"Look Elite you are an amazing woman, any man should be happy to have you. I would be happy to have you," he said causing my head to fly up and my eyes to pop open. He wore a big ass grin until suddenly he was being snatched from his chair by Zir, a gun pressed to his temple.

People started screaming and I knew the cops would be there soon. "Zir, what are you doing," I said hoping he would calm down. Beefing or not I wasn't about to let my man go to jail. "This is my counselor, just put him down and let's go," I cried out grabbing his arm. Muscles and all Paul was no match for Zir's rage. He hit him a few times in the head with the back of his gun then punched him so hard I heard his jaw crack.

"Elite don't fucking tell me what to do while you over here all hugged up with this nigga. Did you forget you were married or just didn't give a fuck? This why you were ending shit wit me? Oh, I see that's why you didn't want me to know about your little pregnancy, it's this nigga baby right," Zir said with hate in his eyes.

"You know what Zir, this your fucking baby, but I wish it wasn't," I screamed at him before I ran out.

Zir

Hearing Elite say that she wished she wasn't having my

baby fucked me up. I didn't even bother going home I just went to the trap and stayed there for a few days. I could have gotten a room or even slid over Alexcia's way, but I didn't want to be bothered with anyone. I sent the workers home and ran that shit just like when I was a lil nigga on the block.

Today I had to go and check on some of my legal businesses, it was time to get back to the real world. I owned a ton of shit that no one knew about but I kept up with. Aside from the barbershop I owned a corner store, two sneaker spots and a nigga even copped a Popeye's last year. Anything I could do to clean up the dirty money I was all about it. This street shit wouldn't last forever.

Pulling away from my Popeye's on Lake Ave all I could do was shake my head. Every girl I had working in there was a freak. I swear these hoes wore the tightest fucking khaki uniform pants you could find. The shirts had so many buttons opened I saw more tittie's than the strip club.

Parking in front of the barbershop I walked inside with my hood on hoping no one bothered me. "Yo Zir, you got a visitor. Shorty been here every day this week just waiting on yo ass," Keen said as I made my way towards my office. Seeing Alexcia leaning against the door gave me an instant migraine.

"Why the fuck you here! You are always here, underfoot, calling me, stalking me. I know my dick was good but God damn girl you aint even had none in years. Your child support was transferred on Friday just like every week. But you still feel the need to come to my spot and lurk around like a sick ass puppy."

I unlocked the door not even waiting for a response. Turning to slam the door behind me her ass was in my way just that fast.

"If you think you're going to close this door in my face and ignore me and your kid you have another thing coming you Punta," she spat at me. "You want to fuck, come home to cooked meals, I got you. I been telling you that but you playing all these games. You weren't dodging me when I was busting it open in Miami but once a baby entered the picture you became the fucking disappearing man."

I noticed everyone staring my way, she had to bring this shit to the hood and to my fucking business. I felt like every chance of keeping this situation from my wife was fading fast. "Look Alexcia I will come to the house in an hour just get out of here. All this shit you talking about my shorty where the fuck she at? You don't even know anyone in this city. Stop coming up here I know what you want. I understand now."

I kissed her on the cheek and turned her around so she could go. "Fuck," I said low as we ran right into Chrome. I was so caught up in planning how I was killing this stupid bitch later that I never even noticed him standing there.

Chrome was pacing my office like he was the one caught up in this shit. "Nigga for real, a baby? I knew you was fucking that bitch when I caught her slick ass up here last time, but you really went in that raw. I never thought you of all people would have gotten caught up with a kid. Elite's going to leave your ass."

"Son it's not even like that. I fucked her ass one time in Miami almost four years ago, shit I don't even think that's my kid. I aint never even have shit to do with the little girl. I already told her she was on her own the minute she cried pregnant because I love my wife."

"You love your wife," Elite said, her voice coming from behind me. She was standing in the doorway with tears streaming down her face. I could see all the pain she was feeling in her eyes and it made me go numb. She ran up and punched me in my shit. Chrome didn't stop her and neither did I. I deserved that and anything else she wanted to do.

"The fucked-up thing was that I could have lived with this. I knew when you were out there cheating day in and day out that a baby was a possibility, but you really lied about this shit all these years? You hid a whole fucking kid?"

"E wait," I called out as she ran out the door.

***

I spent the last two days searching every hotel in the city for Elite. She left the shop that day and came home to pack her bags. Even picked up my kids from my aunt. No one has heard from her since. I knew I fucked up on so many levels and I had to find her and make shit right. I couldn't have shorty out there with my kids going through it. I needed them like I needed air to breathe.

Seeing Alexcia call me back-to-back I hit reject and then block. I knew she was my baby moms, but I wasn't about to deal with her ass on any level. This shit was her fault. If she would have just got a fucking abortion or left me alone my wife and kids would be home where they belonged.

Pacing the floors all I heard was the sound of my Timbs on the hard wood. No one was here to tell me what my next move should be and as a man I never needed anyone to tell me. I knew I fucked up, I really fucked up and there wasn't shit else I could say. I thought about going to kill that nigga she was chatting it up with the other day but that wasn't going to bring my kids home.

Picking up my phone I called a cop I kept on payroll. "Yo Ray, I need you to do something for me. My wife kidnapped my shorty's and I want my fucking kids back. Trace her phone or some shit but I need my little ones home with me like yesterday." After sending him the info he needed I grabbed the bottle of Henny and made my way to the couch. I couldn't do this thing called life without my baby girl. E was all I had in this bitch and if I had to kill every person I saw I would be bringing her home.

Elite

Looking at my phone I didn't want to turn it on because I knew Zir was still blowing me up. Shit him and my mama but since Xay was in the hospital I had to check in with my bestie. Fuck it, I would just ignore them until I was done.

After four rings Kyona finally picked up. Her voice sounded so defeated that I was scared my Godson didn't make it through the night. "Ky how is my baby?"

"He's bad, he has a tube in for breathing and his immune system is attacking itself. E I'm scared he isn't going to be ok. They said this shit came from him having the flu but he wasn't even sick. He had the flu shot this year. I think they just saying stuff because they don't know what the fuck is going on." I didn't even know what to say. I didn't want to bring my situation up to her right now because that wasn't important. I needed to just say fuck hiding out and go be with my best friend.

"Look Ky I'm going to get the kids together and take them to my mom. I will come up there with you as soon as I can. I love you and Xay, he is going to make it through." Ending the call, I looked at my kids sleeping on the king-sized bed. I couldn't imagine the pain Kyona was going through right now. As much as Chrome got on my fucking nerves, I was glad he was there for her. I know he loved Xayden as much as she did.

Hearing a knock on the door I was confused. I had a friend from work put a room at the Hyatt downtown in her name and I gave her cash. So no one knew where I was. No one called out maid service or no shit like that so I just ignored them mother fuckers. The knock came again a few minutes later. Annoyed I called out, "who is it," and got off the chair I was in.

"Ma'am it's the police, open up." My heart started to beat hard as hell. All I could think about was something had happened to Zir. He was a street nigga and the life he lived came with a lot of risk.

Snatching open the door two cops stood there with their badges out. "Elite Bailey?" they asked, and I nodded my head in confirmation. "Ma'am are your children here?" they asked as they stepped inside almost pushing me down.

"Yes, why do you need to know about my children?" I snapped putting my hands on my hips. I knew they could hear the attitude in my voice because the cop with the blond hair looked uncomfortable. I hope they weren't about to kidnap my ass. "Do I need to call a lawyer or maybe nine one one? What the fuck do you want?"

"Please place your hands behind your back. You are under arrest for the kidnapping of Blaise Zir Bailey Jr. and Kyoni Laila Bailey. You have the right to remain silent, anything you say can be used against you in a court of law," he was still talking but my mind was blank. How the fuck did I kidnap my own kids. Feeling the cold steel against my wrists I started to panic. Kicking the black cop as hard as I could I elbowed the other one and ran to where my kids were.

I couldn't even pick my babies up with my hands behind my back but maybe if I could wake Laila up, she could grab ZJ, and we could make a run for it. Mister blonde cop, wanted to be Billy Bad ass and walk up on me. He grabbed my arm hard as a bitch, but before I could fight back, I heard Zir's deep voice.

"Get your hands the fuck off of her before you catch a hot one." He stalked his way over to us and pulled me into his space. I was still mad as hell at him, so I just glared. But lowkey I was happy as hell to see him because I didn't know what was going on.

"Man get this shit off my wife. Ya'll are good. I got what I wanted so I aint pressing charges." The black cop un-cuffed me and Zir handed them a stack each.

"You did this shit? I thought I was being fucking kidnapped or something. What the fuck was the purpose of calling the cops and telling them I kidnapped my children?" I asked as I started hitting him. Lately I been fighting this nigga what seems like all the time.

"Zir for real man, you got us out here on some bogus shit. I thought your girl really stole your kids. Filing false charges on somebody aint not joke," the blonde cop complained. Zir looked at him like he had lost his mind and his partner shoved him out the door.

"You really low nigga. I had all rights to take my kids and leave. We don't need you following behind us or searching for us. Go find your other kid and spend time with her because I'm done." I walked closer to the door hoping he would just get the fuck out. Instead he just stood in front of me staring me down.

"You think you got this shit figured out. Babe I fucked up, I can't lie and I can't go back and fix that shit but I made sure it didn't come your way all these years. I can keep doing that, I made sure you and our kids came first." He stood there like the shit he was saying was making since or even moving me. "E, I never even acknowledged that kid, I wasn't about to let her come in and fuck up what me and you had."

"Don't you ever in your life act like you being a deadbeat dad was a fucking favor to me. You think that ignoring a whole child makes her go away? That she was going to what, someday forget she was supposed to have a dad and shit was going to be, ok"

"I feel like I don't even fucking know you. What if that

little girl was Laila, you would choose to not be her father because of your love for a bitch? What you need to be doing is making this right with your little girl. Try apologizing to your daughter because she needs it. I don't, I'm not even interested in that shit," I folded my arms trying to give myself some space from him.

"E, don't do this ma. I know you aint ask me to turn my back on my shorty but I wasn't about to let you get hurt. Shit a nigga didn't know what to do. Just come home E, I promise I will make this right, wit you and her. I aint got no more secrets, nothing else to hide. I need you." He pulled me into his arms and I swore I felt a tear on my head. I stood there holding my body stiff not wanting to let my guard down. I knew he was just trying to protect me but could I live with the way he did it?

"Zir I was always coming home, shit that's my spot. I just don't know if yo ass gonna be there with me."

Chapter 10

Shaquita

I touched my lip and felt the blood dripping from everywhere. Damn I though Keisha whooped my ass good the other day. Elite went in to straight killer mode. I knew the only reason I wasn't out on my ass yet was the fact that her and Zir were having a damn fist fight about her hiding her pregnancy. I hurried and made my way downstairs hoping I could slide off into the bedroom I was staying in unseen. "Umm, were the fuck do you think you're going little girl," Miss Connie's voice said behind me. She scared the shit out of me.

"To my room," I snapped at her. She was starting to get on my nerves with her miss goody goody act. I knew she was a fucking hoe just like the rest of us. I heard all about her track record. She had a fucking line of men she used to "date", who just fucked her and ducked her. She should be happy my pops was giving her a real chance with his dumb ass.

"Oh, I guess you think I wasn't going to say shit about what you just did. You are a nasty little thing; you would come in here to these people's home. People who offered you a roof over your head and try and fuck up their marriage," she looked at me like I was making her sick. Shit the feeling was mutual so all well. "I'm done with you, make sure by Tuesday you have a place to go because this isn't working. I won't have you here causing my daughter all this stress," she shot at me before turning to walk away. Had she moved any faster that sadly placed lace front would have flew off her fucking head.

I didn't respond because I wasn't worried. My father would make sure I was good, me and the boys. Plus, my child support should be in soon and I would be all set. I didn't need her old raggedy ass. Always trying to act like this was one big happy fucking family. Well, her and her family could go to hell.

Stepping around the boys who I made sleep on some blankets on the floor I climbed in the comfortable king size bed. Grabbing my bullet out of my purse next to the bed I closed my eyes and fantasized about Zir's big dick and how it felt hitting the back of my throat.

After bringing myself to a huge orgasm I didn't even bother to get up and clean my sticky pussy. I was so close to getting Zir's dick and raw at that. He could have been my next baby-daddy, but no. Elite had to keep fucking up all my plans. I still blamed her for Chrome and me not making it. If it wasn't for her bestie I would be his number one bitch. All the sudden along came Kyona and suddenly he was in love. She didn't even have much to offer. She was plain as fuck. Her breasts couldn't be bigger than a C cup and I knew her ass had nothing on mine. I just got it redone four months ago. It was a birthday present to myself courtesy of Shakita's child support check.

Seeing as though I had work the next day I decided to try and get some sleep. I also had a date, and I didn't want to be looking tired starting a new friendship. My new friend Deric was some kind of executive for Frito Lay, I met him on a dating site and I knew he had potential. All I needed was one more baby daddy to add to the team.

Morning came faster than I wanted, but I slept good after my bullet satisfied me last night. I really needed regular dick in my life again. The Advil PM worked too well on the boys they were still knocked out cold on the floor.

Tripping over Boobie's bad ass as I made my way to take

a shower I felt my temper flare. "Get the fuck up," I yelled kicking them both in the ribs. I had to get them to school and me to stupid fucking work. I was able to get myself dressed and ready in thirty minutes but I swore that the kids were moving slower than ever today.

Miss Connie was nowhere to be found to help out and Shakita had already left to be with her father. Snatching Ray Ray by his arm I ignored his cries of pain and shoved him right out the front door. "Boobie, let's fucking go." He came trailing out behind us, shoes untied and milk still around his mouth. I swear these kids where fucking gross.

By the time I dropped them off and made my way to work I was over forty-five minutes late. Sighing I slid my way into the call center and logged on to my system. I saw my manager Julia walk past me several times and I knew she wanted to write me up, but I made sure I stayed on a call so she wouldn't fuck with me.

These customers have been so annoying, and I didn't have the patience for one more stupid ass question. Yet here I was on the phone just trying to walk this old ass lady through opening her e-mail. "Look if you can't figure out how to work an e-mail I can't help you. Why don't you call back when you have someone with you who knows what they are doing," I hung up on her hoping she would call back and get someone else.

"Shaquita, please log off and come to my office. Now," Julia said. Her face was blank but I knew she was pissed off. *Fuck.* As I grabbed my purse and iPhone, I saw the screen light up with a call from Boobies school. What the fuck he do now? Pressing decline, I noticed the ten missed calls with the same number from earlier. They would have to figure that out, I was trying to keep my job.

"Please have a seat," she said as I walked in her office and saw Tammy from HR there. I knew the drill, shit the brown box was waiting on the desk for me to pack up my stuff. I worked in the call center I aint have anything in this bitch anyway.

"Look Julia, Tammy we can all just save each other some time because I see what the fuck ya'll trying to do. Fuck this job, make sure I get my final paycheck and just slide my termination paper work over this way." I stood waiting for that shit as patiently as I could. Tammy looked shocked but Julia had a smirk on her face. I didn't care about either one honestly.

I was going to take the paper showing I was fired to the welfare office and make sure I got more money from them. Working wasn't really for me. I had been pretending to be someone I wasn't and was over it. Snatching my papers from Tammy's hand I headed outside to smoke a fat ass blunt.

I ignored the kid's school a few more times and rode around town most of the day. I wasn't coming in that house early letting my pops know I lost my job. His ass would find out soon enough when snitching ass Elite or Kyona said something. But since neither one of those bitches made it to work today, I was safe for the moment.

***

I decided on a little black dress for my date with Deric and I had to say with my new ass I was killing it. I turned around in the mirror and smoothed my hands over the twenty-inch bundles I had installed last week. Throwing some cherry flavored lip gloss on I was ready to go. As soon as my hand touched the front door my dad walked in the room. "Where the fuck you think you going without your kids," he said looking me up and down like I was some cheap meat.

"Dad I have a date tonight. I told you about it last week and you said no problem." I knew I didn't tell him shit but I was going to pretend I did. He shook his head at me and narrowed his eyes.

"Little girl if you want to go on a date, or to the moon I don't give a fuck. But make sure those kids are by your side because I am done helping you." He looked at the boys and then back to me before getting up and leaving. Fuck it I didn't need his old shady ass anyway.

"Let's go boys. I have a date." I drove all the way to Henrietta mad as a bitch. If I had my own crib I could have left these little gremlins home alone but I would have to improvise. Turning left into the parking lot I saw Deric's red Jeep already there.

Turning to Ray Ray and Boobie I figured I would set some ground rules. "Look, mommy is going in to have dinner so you two better stay in this car and don't fuck with nothing. I will be out when I can, oh and I'm taking the keys." I gave them one last warning look and left them playing on their tablets.

"Hey baby," I cooed as I sat down across from Deric. His ass was sexy, coco brown skin, dimples and a he wore his curly hair in a low cut. A true pretty boy, I met him in the grocery store. He took one look at my body and told me he couldn't live without me. It helped that he had a good job and no kids. He grinned at me as I leaned across the table and licked my lips. I had no idea where those kids were going after this dinner, but I was going to get some dick.

"Shaquita you looking good as fuck girl. What you want to eat, get whatever you want," he said.

"Can I have the shrimp scampi with broccoli on the side? Also, I would like a raspberry tea to drink," I told the waitress who kept looking at me like I was in the wrong spot. Shit maybe she felt like my dress was too short for this fancy ass restaurant but I didn't care. She wasn't buying my meal so fuck her.

The food came and I swear that shit was so good. I had never really been on a date before. Most niggas I messed with just wanted to fuck in the house not take me out places. "Wow who brings their kids to a spot like this and then lets them run around fucking with people's food," Deric said interrupting my happy thoughts. Turning around slowly I prayed a little in my head that it wasn't my kids. How could it be my kids when they were in the car?

"Boobie, Ray Ray," I hissed across the room as I watched them grab bread sticks and desserts from random people's tables. They ran all over playing tag with each other than began throwing the food. *SHIT.*

"Yo those are your kids," Deric asked his voice sounded shocked and pissed.

"Yea they were supposed to stay in the car," I mumbled. Deric pushed his chair back and threw a few hundreds on the table. I watched as he walked out without even saying good-bye. The waitress stood in front of the table laughing behind her hand. "Shut the fuck up," I said as I got up and grabbed my kids. This day was all the way screwed up. I needed a damn do over.

The ride back to Elite and Zir's house was a silent one, I didn't even have the energy to scream at these kids anymore. I wanted to drive the car off the bridge and into the water with them inside but I needed my fucking car. Pulling up at Zir and Elites house I noticed the all black Mazda truck parked in front. Great they had some sort of company, I hope I could just make my way to my room without seeing anyone. Knocking, my father flung open the door with a look on his face I had never saw before.

"Well here she is right now," he said stepping back letting me come in. "Shaquita you have visitors," he said waving his hand towards a lady I had never seen before. She was cute for someone in her thirties, her light skin was complimented by the honey blonde hair she had cut into a bob. She had on tight blue jeans, a black V-neck sweater and a pair of black Hunter boots.

"I'm sorry can I help you?" I asked trying not to have an attitude. Maybe she was some girl my pops was fucking and he wanted me to meet her.

Her face turned a shade of red and her lips twisted into a smirk. "If you wanted to help me you wouldn't have fucked my husband. Now let's cut out all the bullshit. I came for the boy, he will be coming to live with us because I refuse to allow a hoe like you to see a penny more of my money." She looked behind her at a man I hadn't seen in years. "Which one of these brats is yours? Grab him and let's go, I have things to do," she commanded.

Boobies father didn't even bother to speak just pointed him out. How the fuck did his wife get involved in this shit. I couldn't afford to lose another payout from a baby daddy so this wasn't about to happen. Not today. "Bitch it's not my fault that your nigga was raw dogging me. Now he has to pay for his mistakes. You won't be taking anything out of here. This is my fucking son."

"Was he your son when the school couldn't find you today? They had to call child protective services, then they had to find the father on record after they couldn't find you. We have papers for him and he is coming with us. I have found a nice boarding school for his little ass. He won't be corrupting my kids. Now it's time to go." She grabbed Boobie by the hand, his father already had his bags and just like that they were gone. How they even get my son's shit?

Turning to look at my dad he just stood there, like he was in shock. "You need to go, I have already packed your stuff and it is in the hall waiting. I will help with Ray Ray until you can get you a place and all but I am done with you. I get you a job and you get fired. You are fucking all these married men, not taking care of your kids. What kind of person are you? You know what don't even answer that, just get the fuck out," he opened the front door ready for me to leave. I grabbed my things and headed out, turning around to see if he was for real I was met with the front door slamming in my face.

Keisha

"Ma, I got to get Shakita into school and all that shit. You gonna help a nigga out?" Ju stood in front of me looking good as fuck. All I could think about was how it felt sleeping in bed next to him last night. His big ass dick was pressed against my ass and I swear I didn't sleep at all. I could barely follow what he was saying.

"Sure you know I got you. I went and bought her some new clothes and shoes yesterday since she had outgrown the stuff you had here for her." Shakita had some clothes from living with her grandfather but they were mostly Walmart brand. I wasn't going to have my kids walking around in Polo and she was wearing two-dollar shirts.

"Yea, that's what I love about you shorty you always good to my kids," he said with a half-smile. He leaned down and kissed me on the lips. I was stunned because he usually didn't do shit like that. I guess he was just grateful I was helping him with his daughter. I was in love with him and didn't want him to be grateful, I wanted him to return my feelings.

Jerking my head away I got up so I could go register Shakita at the same Montessori school that Cadence was enrolled in. "Damn ma it's like that," he said to my back. I just shook my head. I didn't want to get into it with him. I was thankful he was allowing me to stay with him until I got into my own place, but I wasn't about to complicate shit. Getting my feelings involved only to get them hurt all over again would be a big mistake. He still looked at me as Shaquita's ratchet friend. He probably thought I was out to get him for his money like she was. I wished I had someone else growing up to be friends with, or that I was an Elite or Kyona, classy and in high demand.

"Shakita, get ready baby we are about to go to your new school," I called out. I knew he wouldn't keep asking me shit in front of her. Looking in on lil Ju he was in his bedroom playing with the million toys his dad had bought him. "Come on fats let's get dressed," I said as I picked him up and tickled him. I ignored Ju as he followed me around the room like he had some shit he wanted to say or do.

"I'm ready," Shakita called as she bounced into the room with a smile on her face. I had braided her hair straight down her back and she had some barrettes on the ends. Her smile was infectious causing me to grin back. "Can we have donuts on the way, please," she asked spinning around and falling on the floor causing Ju to laugh and clap his hands?

"Of course we can," I answered. With all the abuse she had been through I couldn't believe how happy she was. I was honestly surprised that Shaquita wasn't dead once me and Ju heard all the things she was doing to Shakita. I knew she was using her kids for a check but I never thought she was mistreating them the way she was. If I ever saw her ass again it was going to be a beat down on site.

"Take your brother in the front for a few minutes to play. Keisha will be out soon," Ju commanded. Watching her carry the baby to the front I leaned against the dresser waiting for what was coming next. "Here is the money for the tuition and whatever else you need," he said handing me a stack of hundred dollar bills.

"Cool I will bring back what is left," I responded as I grabbed it and tried to move around him.

"Where the fuck you going?" he asked. "You act like a nigga can't kiss you now. What you not fucking with me," he said as he used his body to pin mine to the dresser. My pussy was leaking but my heart was on high alert, telling me to run away. His teeth bit my neck gently and I felt my body tense up. "I know you want this so why you fighting it?"

"Julian, I have feelings for you, feelings that you don't share so I think we should just keep shit simple. I don't want to be here fucking you, allowing my heart to get involved and then hating you when you move on to the next. We got kids so we have to hold this shit together." I gently pushed him but he didn't budge. The last thing I remembered before my pants dropped was him shoving his tongue down my throat.

Chapter 11

Kyona

I just stared at the nurse. I was speechless, she just told me my son may not make it through the night and I couldn't even find the words to express how I felt. "This is from the flu?" I asked in a stutter. "He got a flu shot. He didn't even have a fever." My voice sounded crazy, high pitched and out of control which was how I felt.

"Fuck that our son is making it through the damn night. Don't even put that negative shit in the air. Go get me a new nurse. I don't want you around my shorty." I could tell by how Chrome sounded he was close to losing it too. "Come here don't start thinking that shit. We are not losing our son." He put his arms around me and held me close. I listened to the sound of his heart beat and tried to calm down. This all happened so fast, I still wondered what I could have done differently.

"My mom will be coming to get the baby since we can't get in touch with Elite. Then we gonna stay here with Xay until he is better." He was trying to reassure me and it was sweet.

"Chrome, I know you have business to handle and shit, you don't have to sit up here," I said giving him an out. I couldn't see Xayden's real father even sitting up here so I didn't expect Chrome to do it. Suddenly I felt something hot like my hair was being ripped from my scalp.

"This not the time for your bullshit. You knew I wasn't about to leave you or Xay but you had to say some slick shit.

I'm yo nigga and this my son and I aint going any fucking where. Now act right." My eyes were leaking from the shit he just pulled but he was right. I couldn't stop my mouth that was how I was built.

Sinking down next to the bed I began praying to God to save my son's life. I must have sat there for a while with my eyes closed and my heart shattered just talking to God. "Really Serino this is how I find out I have a grand-child," I heard Chrome's mother say. Popping my head up I gave an ashamed smile. I thought he would have told her by now but I should have a long time ago.

"Both of you are in trouble but not now, this isn't the time. Once Xay is all better and up running around I will have some words for the two of you." She grabbed Serina and put her coat and hat on. "Come on grandma baby. I may never let you go I have been waiting on my own grans for so long." She glared at us, leaned over and kissed Xayden, then left.

"Well we are both on her bad side," I said causing Chrome to give me his sexy half smile. Sitting in the stiff hospital chair we settled in to watch our son throughout the night.

***

Two days later Xayden had made it through the worst. Or at least that's what the doctors told me. I didn't trust shit they had to say at this point. I watched my son shake, fight to breathe, run fever after fever and damn near swallow his tongue from a seizure. I didn't know if I will ever feel like he is ok again. Hell, I would probably never feel comfortable leaving his side again. I watched Chrome sleep with Xay's hand in his. He didn't leave at all, he rejected all calls once he let his cousin know what was up and gave me all his attention and support.

I wasn't sure I could really let him go, he was the man I

loved but he had moved on. It was probably too late. Stepping into the bathroom I slightly closed the door so I could call my job. I had no idea when I would be back in and they needed to replace me for the upcoming training class.

"I'm sorry but there is no way I can make it in to work for the upcoming training class. My son is in the hospital and I refuse to leave his side," I explained to my boss Penny. I knew these mother fuckers wasn't stressing me about they funky ass job. I looked at the phone with a mug on my face. No matter what my kids would always come first so she could go play in traffic. Shit I remember when Penny's son got drunk and hit a pole, she was out for three months taking care of him. I had been gone less than a week.

"Well Kyona you have been out for several days and unfortunately since you cannot make it in-" that was all I heard because Chrome had snatched the phone out of my hand. I didn't even hear him come in behind me.

"You know what, fuck your job she don't need it anyway." He hung up and handed it back to me. "Kyona, don't ever beg a motherfucker about shit. You got me so you don't need them. Our kids always come first, and you never had to work to begin with. As long as I'm out here breathing I got ya'll." I licked my lips and prepared a speech in my head. I knew I had to let him know he didn't have to take care of anyone but the kids. Shit really not even them.

He stalked me, moving closer and closer until my back was against the door. "Shorty it's like you don't get this shit. I see the wheels turning in your head and I know you bout to say something to piss me off. You belong to me, I can't let you go even if I wanted to. Even when you say you not with me you still mine. I love you and I'm always going to take care of you, put you before me. Now stop all that crying shit."

His lips gently kissed mine. I guess he didn't care about the new girl he was with and if he didn't care, neither did

I. Not now, almost losing Xayden showed me life is fragile. I wasn't going to make him suffer anymore. I had to forgive him because I loved him, and the reality was I could lose him at anytime. I wasn't going to live with any regrets.

Chrome

Watching my son suffer the past few days had me more than fucked up. I can't lie and say I didn't cry, even though Xayden wasn't my blood he was mine and I wasn't about to lose him to no fucking cold. If I was an ignorant nigga, I would have blamed his mama when she didn't look further into him not feeling well, but I knew in my heart this shit wasn't her fault. I watched her blame herself more than I ever could. All I could do was hold her and wipe her tears.

The way I saw her give up her job when it came to our son made me love her more if that was possible. I wasn't ever letting baby girl go. I could tell she was more than stressed but I was going to do all I could to take that shit away.

"Ky just go in there and worry about Xay, everything else is on me." Kissing her on the cheek I walked her back into the hospital room. I was about to make sure she ate something because she had barely been eating shit since we been here and I didn't need my girl fading away.

Skipping the cafeteria crap I hopped in my car and made my way to Popeye's. Checking my phones, I had too many missed calls to ever catch up on. Jayda started blowing me up again, I hadn't checked in with shorty since the day I dropped her ass off after work. "Yo," I answered as I pulled into the drive through lane.

"That's how you answer me? Where the fuck you been? Me and you supposed to be rocking together and you just drop the fuck out of my life. I know you think your money makes you special but it doesn't. I deserve respect, you fucking me so that means you need to be answering to me when I hit you up." I put her ass on mute and ordered my baby mom her food. She was going hard and I swear I was laughing. Her ass didn't even stop to take a breath, no wonder her head skills was so good.

"Jayda look if you done with all that bullshit, I'm about to hang up ma. Go find a new nigga to bother I got some family shit going on and I already told you no one comes before my kids and they mom. Just do us both a favor and lose my number. And as a piece of advice if you think you deserve respect stop fucking niggas the day you meet them." I could hear her screaming as I clicked end. Blocking her ass, I sat in the car for a few minutes after parking in the hospital garage. I needed that time to get myself together because I had to be strong for Ky, she didn't need to know I was scared too.

VALENTINES DAY

Chapter 12

Elite

I woke up once I heard movement in the bedroom. I wasn't really feeling Valentine's Day this year but the breakfast tray with homemade cards from my babies brought a smile to my face. Even though me and Zir seemed to be back on track it was just a front. We slept in the same bed since I had been home, but only spoke if it was concerning the kids. He kept wanting me to hear him out, but I just wasn't there yet. He had done more than hurt me, I was disappointed.

I couldn't let him not be a father to Isabella. Just the fact that he so easily ignored one of his children for any bitch, even if it was me changed the way I saw him as a man. I couldn't shake it off because if he could do that to one innocent child he could do it to mine. Plus as his wife I felt like I had a responsibility to this child as well. It made me feel guilty, especially as I watched him around here being the perfect fucking father to ours.

We just couldn't see eye to eye. He maintained he didn't even know if that was his kid but anyone with eyes could look and see how much she looked like Laila. That was just a lame ass excuse, if he didn't know he should have fucking found out. It wasn't shit to go get a test done. That should have been his first fucking step. What if she wasn't his and his dumb ass been stressing and paying for a kid all this time.

I could tell this pregnancy was going to be a bitch. Physically I was exhausted all the time and suffering from morning sickness. I wasn't really worried about the post-partum shit as much anymore. I found a new therapist, this time one who wasn't trying to fuck me on the low and she had helped a lot. I had been holding my emotions in check even though the problems with my husband had left me feeling all alone in the world.

"You not getting up," Zir asked while sitting on the end of the bed. I had finished my food a while ago and even though I knew he always did Valentine's Day big I wasn't backing down. He could go spend the day with another bitch the way I was feeling. If he couldn't figure out shit with his other child, I was good.

"What the fuck I'm getting up for," I asked with an attitude. I made sure to roll my neck and my eyes before turning my attention back to the TV.

"Here man at least get these gifts with your spoiled ass," he said throwing a bunch of bags on the bed. I wasn't turning down any gifts so I tore into the bags. There was a diamond bracelet with a matching pair of earrings inside velvet black boxes. A pair of Gucci sneakers and a matching shirt and a Louis Bag. The last bag had two bikinis, sun screen and a stuffed Mickey Mouse. What the fuck, it was two feet off snow outside what was I about to do with a damn swimsuit and sun block.

"Zir I aint going on no fucking trip with yo ass. I aint going no fucking where with you, so you can take this shit back," I said throwing the bag his way.

He left the room but didn't seem mad. Shit maybe he just didn't give a fuck anymore. I was starting to feel that way too.

"Laila, Isabella, come on," he called out as he came back in the room with ZJ in his arms. Laila bounced in behind him followed by a pretty little girl that I recognized from the pictures in his phone. She smiled shyly and then stood behind his legs. "Mommy doesn't want to go to Disney World with us," he said giving the kids a puppy dog face. They all looked at me like I was the monster from under the bed.

"I didn't say that," I slowly said, calming them down. Immediately they started jumping up in down in excitement.

He winked at them as he made his way closer to me. He spoke so only I could hear, the girls were lost in their own world, making vacation plans. "Listen bae you were right, about everything. I can't take back anything I did all I can do is make it right going forward. I still love you more than anything or anyone but I wasn't being a man."

"Leaving my shorty out there without a pops was a bitch move and I thank God I have a woman like you that wouldn't let me get away with it." He stopped for a minute, and I saw a look of pain cross his face. "I had the test done, she is mine, and once her mom found out I wasn't going to be with her she bounced." I had to coach myself to breathe, it could have been worse, she could have kept Isabella from us. I wouldn't turn my back on her. She was a part of my husband, and she was my kid's sister. We would make it work.

I got on my knees and wrapped my arms around him. "Thank you, this is the best Valentines Day gift ever," I whispered. He wasn't perfect but he was mine. Today and always.

Chapter 13

Shaquita

I woke up to the loud ass beeping of some truck backing up and chains being rattled. Sleeping in my car sucked but I was able to move in to my new apartment today so I wasn't sweating it. I knew I fucked up, but my father putting me out of the house was ridiculous. He was always acting so proper and perfect. He worked his good nine to five as some financial advisor, went to church and barely uttered a curse word. Well fuck him, where was all that perfection when my mother was letting men touch my little young body for crack. He never saved me and he knew what my life was like. I guess I didn't fit into his perfect mold.

My car suddenly jerked and then began moving. Jumping out I realized it was hooked to the chains I had heard and being lifted by a tow truck onto a flat bed. "What the hell are you doing? This is my fucking car you idiot and I was in it." I didn't care which one of Connie's nosey ass neighbors were looking.

"Ma'am we got the call from the owners of this home stating a car was illegally parked in their driveway. Are you aware this is private property? What were you doing in there anyway? Sleeping?" he asked with his nose turned up. This dude was giving me the look people used to give my mother when she would walk around in dirty clothes, her hair not combed.

"Look this is my father's house he was just throwing a tantrum about something irrelevant. So you can put the car down and keep it moving. Thanks," I added with a snotty tone. I didn't give a fuck that I probably looked homeless and hadn't brushed my teeth or washed my face yet. I knew my body was still the shit and he had better treat me like it.

"We will drop the car for the same two-hundred-dollar fee that you had to pay to get it out. If you wait twenty four hours the charge goes up. Shit it's your choice I'm just here doing my job and really doing you a favor by not taking it to the yard." He leaned against the truck and lit a cigarette looking bored. I stood there staring for a while, but he was unmoved. "Honey you got until this smoke is done to make a choice. I have other cars to pick up."

This corny ass redneck was serious. I looked him up and down, he was out here in this cold ass air without a coat just his red flannel shirt. His beard was so dingy I swore a fly raced out that bitch a minute ago. Going back inside my car I rifled through my bag getting the cash. Throwing it at him I stood back and waited until the car was lowered to the ground. My shit hit the ground with a thud and he smirked at me from the window of his truck before he pulled off.

I wasn't worried about that little money. My child support should be showing today from Ray Ray's dad. At least I still had that income. The extra money would see me through since I didn't have to financially support as many kids. Shit no kids if my dad kept Ray Ray.

My stomach was on fire from hunger so I decided to go and grab me a turkey sub and a Pepsi from the spot in the hood. Maybe I would meet a new "friend" there. Hood rich niggas stayed hanging out on the block. Pulling up I double parked so I could run in. It was too cold to be doing anymore walking than necessary. "Yo Abdul make me a large Turkey sub, mayo, lettuce, oil and lots of tomatoes." I went to grab my Pepsi's in a can just the way I liked em and made my way to the register.

"The total is thirteen dollars and seventy-five cents," he said, and I slid my EBT card. Typing the pin in I waited for the receipt but the shit beeped and rejected popped up on the screen.

"Run it again, maybe I messed up the pin." Shit it was one two three four so it wasn't really something I should be getting wrong but I popped a few molly's last night so you never know. I performed the process all over again only for the boy behind the counter to shake his head no.

"It says your balance is fifty-four cents, so you don't got enough food stamps," he said sarcastically like the shit was cute. Snatching my card out of the machine I threw down the cash and grabbed my bag. What the fuck, my benefits should have been on the card since the tenth. Stomping my way to the car I threw my stuff inside and sat down in the driver's seat.

The first thing I did was dial the eight hundred number on the back of the card and confirm that my total really was fifty-four cents. This shit had to be a glitch. I called my worker but as always I got a voice mail so I left a message as I drove to my new apartment. Pulling up I was relieved to see the landlord's car in the driveway. I was exhausted from all the stress and I couldn't take anything else today.

"Hello Miss Patty," I called as I got out of the car. She waved back but didn't seem excited to see me. I really didn't give a fuck I just wanted my keys so I could be in my own space.

"Hello Shaquita, I know you were expecting to get your keys today, but I did not get the security deposit or rental agreement from the Department of Human Services. Maybe you can sort all of this out with your worker and let me know what is going on. I can give you until Friday before I rent to the next person on the list." She seemed annoyed, like she was the one being inconvenienced when I didn't have a fucking place to go.

I didn't even respond just jumped in my car sighing because now I had to go to the damn welfare office and wait all freaking day. Pulling up my Bank of America app I logged in to see how much I had because I needed to rent a room for now. My balance was only seventy-seven dollars and six cents. Why was Raymond playing with my damn child support check? He was never late because he didn't want to hear my fucking mouth in his words. Picking up the phone I dialed his number but was sent straight to voice mail.

"Raymond, if you do not send my fucking money now I am going to post pictures of your little dick all over the internet. Then I am going to drop Ray Ray's ass off on your doorstep. Kids aren't cheap or free you stupid mother fucker." I slammed my phone down on the seat next to me. Driving across town I made it to St. Paul St. in silence. I had checked my phone at least twenty times hoping this nigga hit me back with an explanation or something but my shit was dry.

As soon as I pulled into the tiny ass parking lot, they had for us to park in I could feel my annoyance level rise. After circling the lot a few times I was able to steal a spot and park. I made sure to empty my pockets and leave my purse in the trunk. The metal detectors were a bitch and there was no telling what I had in my bag. Sitting on the hard plastic chair I held my number B33 and waited, then waited some more. After three hours my name was finally called. I made my way to the back with a smile because I knew that my day was finally going to turn around.

"Shaquita, do you know that lying to the government on your welfare application is a crime?" The balding white man asked me as he looked over his files in front of him. I could tell he was looking through me rather than at me. His body was slouched over his desk, his attitude made it seem like he was bored out of his mind with his job. I was just a number to him, not even a real person.

"I understand what you are saying sir. I am here because my food stamps are not on my card and my rental voucher wasn't paid for my new apartment. If we can just straighten this all up I will be out of your hair." I was being as nice as I could be considering my freaking day was one straight out of hell.

"I don't think you understand what I'm saying. I'm telling you, young lady that you were investigated for misuse of benefits. You were collecting money from the government for a child that was no longer in your care. That is fraud and it also means you lose your benefits. Getting help from the government is a privilege not a right. Once we have recouped all of the money that you unfairly collected you can reapply for benefits. If you don't have any questions I can walk you out." He stood up letting me know that any questions I had wouldn't make a difference.

I walked out of that building feeling like I couldn't breathe, the cold air filled my lungs as I gasped and coughed. This couldn't be happening to me. Angry and for the first time in a long time feeling panicked, I started my car up and drove to the car lot that Raymond owned. He was going to really have to come up with some money for me. Shit he was my only baby father left that I could still use as a pay day. I parked right in the front of his business, slamming my breaks on. I didn't care if he had customers or not I wouldn't be there long.

Looking around I didn't see any movement and that was strange. The inside lights were out and the place looked abandoned. Slowly I walked up to the front door but when I pulled it, it was locked. There was a white slip of paper taped to the glass. It stated that the property was seized by the police department. I couldn't catch a break, if his business was shut down then where the hell was he? Looking around for a clue to what happened I noticed the bum who always hung out in the front.

"Hey, do you know what happened to the shop," I asked as I approached him. He continued drinking his beer like I wasn't saying shit. Pulling out my last five dollars in cash I handed it to him.

"Well thank you pretty lady," he said smiling showing me he aint have no teeth in his mouth. I tried not to gag as I waited for him to tell me what I wanted to know. "That Ray, he got picked up by the police. He was selling those cars that had already been in an accident like they were brand new. He is going to be locked up for quite a while so if he was your man, find a new one." He laughed, his voice sounding crackly and gross.

"Thank you," I mumbled as I walked away. Picking up the phone I dialed my last chance. Even though he hadn't been answering my calls I knew a way to get his attention. The phone rang a few times and I thought he was going to ignore me but then I heard him breathing on the other end.

"What do you want Shaquita? Do I have to call the police, get a restraining order or some shit? I mean your pussy was good but I'm all set now ma." EJ sounded pissed at the sound of my voice.

"EJ that's no way to treat your baby momma. I'm pregnant boo and it's yours. Now how much you got for me to keep it from that pretty wife of yours?" I could feel my hand itching from the money I was about to get from this nigga.

Instead of a confirmation of funds all I heard was his laughter. He laughed so much he sounded damn near hysterical. "Girl you aint having my baby you sneaky bitch. I had a vasectomy three years ago. I can't have anymore kids. Now go find your baby father and don't fucking call this number no more."

I sat there listening to the dial tone in my ear. My dad would have to help me because now I had no one. Turning the key my car wouldn't turn over. Trying again I heard a bang, and I knew this shit was over. No car, no money and no place to go. I used to have everything and now I was left with nothing, on Valentine's Day.

Keisha

Tucking my legs under me I curled up on the couch and watched the news. I still couldn't believe I was seeing Cesear's face all over the headlines. They found his body mutilated and dumped on a one-way street the night before. I wondered if those guys who were after him finally caught his ass or if he died at the hand of Ju.

I felt some kind of way because I had been with Cesear for what seemed like forever. But the fact that he left me and my kids to be killed because of his nonsense helped me get over his death rather quickly.

The door opened and Ju strolled in, watching him I had to admit I enjoyed my time here with him and all the kids. It felt like we were a family but I knew it was all pretend. "What you doing in here girl," he said as he sat on the couch next to me.

"Just watching TV. The kids are all playing in the back so I was relaxing a little. You want me to make you some breakfast?" I asked him but he shook his head. "I will be out of your hair in two more days. My place will be ready then. Shakita can come with me if you want, I know you got business to handle plus taking care of a little girl is a lot of work. I can't picture you doing hair or homework," I giggled at the thought of him trying to do a ponytail.

"Just like that huh ma? You just come in here and use a nigga for his dick and then bounce." Me and Ju had been fucking like rabbits ever since the day I signed Shakita up for school. That was one of the reasons I was happy to leave. I had gotten comfortable being close to him, of feeling his arms around me as he held me close at night. He sighed before leaning his head back on the couch.

"What's wrong Ju, you looking stressed. Shit I thought you would be happy to see us go. I know you used to having your own space and shit. I'm sure the bitches you fuck are missing you right now." I was being a little petty but I didn't care.

"Naw Keisha, I don't want you to go. I like having you and my kids around. Just stay here, it's more than enough room. Shit you can have your own room if you don't want to fuck with the kid. I'm saying for real though, don't leave." I was confused because I didn't expect this from him.

"Ju, I love being here with you, but that's the problem. I love you and I don't want to get hurt since you don't feel the same. I can't take being hurt like that. So, I have to go, this is what is best for both of us."

I avoided his gaze because I didn't want him to see how in love with him, I really was. Or how much it was going to hurt me to leave. His ass would probably say some shit that would make me feel worse than I already did. Kindness wasn't Julian's strong traits.

"So why I can't be the man who loves you?" he asked. "What a nigga like me can't love anyone? I thought you knew me better than that. Of course I love you, you think I bought yo ass a BMW just because? The amount of money I give you is triple what I gave Shakita's mom."

"You think buying me shit or giving me money means you love me? That's not love. I wanted to be your girl. I wanted to be your girl since the first day I met you, at nine years old. I knew even then that you were the man for me. But you treated me like I was just another bitch in the streets.

It never got better over the years,I was just another Shaquita. So, don't act like you are the victim here or I'm confused." I could feel myself getting loud because he was pissing me the fuck off. Just like I knew he would.

I guess I was doing the same to him because he snatched me by my shirt and pulled me on top of him. I was so close I could smell his toothpaste. "Shorty you are my girl stop acting fucking stupid. You think I got random hoes in my crib. If I wasn't serious about you, I would have dropped you off at the first hotel and kept going. I don't do shit I don't want to do. I aint built like that. If I wanted my kids and not you I would have just murdered you and dropped your body in the street next to Cesear's." He casually shrugged after that statement. "I'm not a sucka ass nigga. How was I going to be with yo ass when you had a fucking man?"

"Yea I can see it by the look on your face that you hadn't thought about that. Ma fucking wit you was never a mistake. I wanted you that's why I bust in yo pussy and made sure you got pregnant. If you didn't tell Cesear about our son I was just going to kill his ass and take you anyway. Now go call them people and tell them you don't need they place you good. Then look on the bed I bought you something to put on we about to go out." He bit the hell out of my bottom lip and literally shoved me off the couch.

I got up to go and handle my business. Trying to figure out Ju was truly a mystery. He could have had me years ago instead he played this game. Letting me stay with a nigga who I didn't want anymore. Looking on the bed I let out a gasp when I saw the white silky dress that was laid out. Next to it was a shoe box from Christian Louboutin and a black velvet box. I stood there in shock looking at the silver necklace that held a heart shimmering in diamonds. Getting dressed I wondered where he was taking me and what I was going to do with the kids. Aside from school and daycare I didn't have too many babysitters.

Looking in the mirror over the dresser I pulled my hair up into a French bun and used some bobby pins to hold it in place. I felt something I had never felt before. I felt special. "Girl you look good as fuck, we may not even make it out the house," Ju said standing in the doorway. As good as his dick was we didn't have to go anyplace. "Come on we aint got time for that right now. My aunt is here to pick up the kids."

Following him I felt my palms sweat. I never met a man's family. Cesear never offered to introduce me to his family and really, I didn't give a fuck. I didn't know Julian had any family close by. He didn't talk about them. "Aunt Kim this is my girl Keisha, Keisha this is my Aunt Kim. The kids are all packed and ready to go," he said to a middle-aged lady who stood there with a wide smile.

She came over and hugged me. I swear she smelled like home-made cookies. It was hard to believe he had this cute little lady who just screamed home and comfort as an aunt, and he was a damn serial killer. Literally. Shaking my head to keep from laughing at the irony I thanked her for helping with the kids. "The girls shouldn't give you any problems but lil Ju is a handful. I hope he doesn't break anything." I was re-thinking this whole sending my kids away for the day idea.

"My son is a boss, if he breaks some shit I will replace it. Now stop worrying before I take back that dress you got on. You gonna be walking in this restaurant butt ass naked," he warned. His aunt didn't seem fazed by what he said at all. She smirked and we walked out behind her. I swear my kids didn't even look back at me. I thought they would cry or something but they were all smiles like I didn't exist.

After driving for a while we passed a bunch of restaurants but he never stopped. Just kept driving until I fell asleep. "We here ma," he shook me awake as we pulled up to some cottage looking place in the middle of nowhere. Slowly I got out of the car and noticed the rose petals leading up to the front door. He held my hand and led me up the walk way.

As his hand went to open the door I hesitated. "Ju you brought me out here to kill me, didn't you?" I asked with uncertainty in my voice.

"Girl bring yo scary ass inside. Only thing getting murdered today is that pussy." Looking in the cabin I felt my tears fall as I saw the candlelight dinner in the middle of the room. I couldn't believe he did all of this shit for me. "Happy Valentine's Day Keish," he said wiping my tears away.

Chapter 14

Kyona

"Ky please go home and get some rest. I promise I won't leave his side. He won't even be in here that much longer, a few more days the doctor said. Just take a shower and change your clothes or something, you will feel better," Chrome said trying to convince me to leave the hospital. I hadn't been in my house for over a week. I had no plans of leaving the hospital without Xayden not even for a second.

Seeing his eyes flutter open I leaned closer to my baby and kissed his forehead. "Xay you ok? Mommy is right here," I reassured him. It was a miracle he made it through the doctors said. I never thought that life could be so fragile even with all I had been through. I had never thought something as common as the flu could almost cost my baby his life. Running my hands through his curls I didn't respond to Chrome. I knew he wouldn't leave Xay, shit he hadn't yet but what if I left and he got bad again.

"Mommy I want you to go home and shower like daddy said. I'm ok now and I'm not a baby. Can you bring me back mister mittens though?" Xayden asked giving me his puppy dog eyes. I swear Chrome was giving me the same look.

"Ok you both win, really Xayden won," I threw in letting Chrome know he wasn't running shit. "I will be back in two hours, that will give me enough time to change clothes, shower and clean up a little." I didn't waste any time. I damn near ran out of the building because the faster I went the faster I could get back.

Being inside seemed odd since it was so quiet. Having two small kids meant it was usually never silent. Setting my purse down I made my way upstairs and fell face down on my bed. I cried and cried until I had nothing left in me. I had been holding so much inside because I was trying to be as strong as I could for Xay but having a moment alone I couldn't hold that shit back anymore. Hugging my pillow, I thanked God again for saving my son and soaked the material in a river of tears.

I must have fallen asleep because I woke up a few hours later and it was almost dark. *Shit.* Throwing my clothes off I scrambled around looking for my phone so I could check in with Chrome. "You look good like that," a male voice said from the other side of the room. I grabbed my chest as I screamed. Tyler stepped out of the shadows, his handsome face was blank and in his hand he had my phone. "Looking for this," he taunted holding the iPhone in his palm.

"What the hell are you doing in my house and with my shit." I reached for my phone, and he called himself grabbing me. I wasn't about to go through this shit with no nigga ever again.

"No bitch where the hell you been is the question!" he said as he held onto my arm tighter. "You don't call, come home, nothing. I told you when I left last time not to fucking play with me!" He looked like a rabid dog with foam coming from his mouth and his eyes blood shot red. It was crazy since he had on some business slacks and a button-down shirt and his favorite vest. It was like Mister Rodgers gone whacky.

"Tyler, we are dating, you don't own me. Let me fucking go and give me my phone. Then get the hell out of my house. I didn't let you in old psycho ass." I didn't waste any more time going back and forth with him. I punched him in his face with my free hand and when he let go of me I hurried to get the glass vase I kept on my dresser. After slamming it into his head and watching it shatter, he fell to the ground.

I should have been scared but instead I was just mad. I had already been through so much and now this. I wasn't about to take anything else lying down. He was bloody but alive. Taking my foot, I began kicking him uncontrollably.

"I hate yo stupid ass. You better get away from me before I kill you," I yelled as I looked around for something to finish him off with. Seeing the iron I had left out I went and grabbed it. Instead of smashing his face in I wrapped the cord around his neck and began strangling him. He clawed at my arms, but I didn't quit. Banging his head on the wall a few times and he stopped. My hands were getting tired but I held on.

"Kyona, you ok," Chrome's voice called from downstairs.

"I'm ok now," I replied as he made his way to me. Looking at the blood all over he shook his head and laughed.

"Damn remind me not to piss you off," he said picking me up off the floor. "Before you say some off the wall shit my mom is with him. I got worried because you were gone all day. Just go shower and shit, I got this." He kicked Tyler so hard in his ribs I could hear the crunch. I trusted Chrome to take care of that mess. I didn't even feel bad for anything I had done or that was going to happen. Running a bubble bath, I sunk into the tub and closed my eyes.

I sat in the tub until Chrome came for me. I didn't want to know what he did to Tyler. My water was cold as hell and my fingers had shriveled from me being in there so long. "Babe you aight?" he asked as I drained the water.

"Yea I'm good now that you are here," I said as I started the shower so I could wash my body good. He started taking his clothes off and got under the hot water with me.

I wrapped my arms around him and let my head rest on his chest. I wished this moment could last forever. Gently I placed a kiss on his chest. I wanted to find a way to tell him I still loved him.

"Shorty you aint got to say shit, I know you love me." He lifted my head up so I could look in his eyes. "You going to give me another chance now," he said low. I could hear in his voice how afraid he was to ask me that shit. He didn't want to hear no.

"Yes I will, don't fuck it up this time." I slowly kissed him on the lips, sucking on his tongue. I missed feeling him inside of me, I swear his dick was like crack. I had to have it. Pinning me to the wall he gave me just what I was craving. "Yes baby this your pussy," I moaned as he bounced me up and down on his dick. I knew I wasn't going to last long the way he was using his free hand to pinch my nipples. That shit had me hot. I came two times back to back and felt my body go limp.

"Naw you aint finished yet," he said talking shit. He turned me over and I braced myself on the wet tiles. Grabbing my waist, he was fucking my ass up. I was trying to run but there was nowhere to go so I had to take the D. "Throw that shit back on me." I eased forward then popped on the tip of his dick. I could tell it was driving him crazy. Finally, he held me in one spot and started digging in my guts. I knew the moment he was about to nut because his whole body went stiff. He let off deep inside me and I tried not to think about the fact I wasn't on any birth control.

"I hope you don't think this is your real Valentine's Day," he said as we rinsed and stepped out. "You get a do over. I was taking you to Venice, I had a whole bunch of romantic shit planned out. Your gifts are still at the crib just waiting on you."

"Chrome I got the best gift of all, you."

125

The End

Made in the USA
Middletown, DE
01 March 2022

61906306R00076